Murder is an Artform

Patricia Fisher Mystery Adventures

Adventures

Book 9

Steve Higgs

Dedication

While writing this book I was spotted – identified as the author who writes these books by a person I do not know. I guess I figured it would happen one day, but this was the first time, and I was left rather speechless.

That lady is Gerry Golding, and this book is dedicated to her.

Thank you for being a fan of my characters.

Table of Contents

Is Anyone Missing a Lobster?

Lunch Date

August Skies

Twisted Relationships

Dinner with Friends

Suicide

Early Clue

Compelling Evidence

Interview with an Innocent Woman

Autopsy Report

An Important Phone Call

It Looked Different in the Pictures

Secret Phone

There is Such a Thing as Too Distracting

A Secret Well Kept

Narcissistic Pig

A History of Violence

Rude Awakening

Unpleasant Scene

News to Shock With

Accusations

Fighting with a Friend

Fond Farewell

Breakfast and a Breakthrough

On the Run

Search for a Killer

Bang to Rights

Return of a Friend

Old Enemy

By the Light of the Moon

Why Lie?

Visitors

Race to Save an Innocent Pig

Back in Dublin

Theories

A Favour Returned

The long Route to the Truth

Change of Venue

Author's notes:

What's next for Patricia Fisher?

A FREE Rex and Albert Story

More Cozy Mystery by Steve Higgs

More Books by Steve Higgs

Free Books and More

Is Anyone Missing a Lobster?

'How long have we got, Mrs Fisher?' Sam's voice reached my ears as a hushed whisper.

The answer, I knew without looking at my watch was more than enough time provided we were not on a wild goose chase. To answer him, I whispered back from the side of my mouth. 'We'll be okay if he turns up soon.'

Sam Chalk is my assistant. He is coming up on his thirty-first birthday and has a shock of brown hair that always starts the day looking neat, but rarely makes it to lunchtime without becoming an unruly mop. Sam has Downs Syndrome, and it makes him very special to me. He sees the world differently from anyone else I know. He has a perpetual smile, a cheeky face, and a willingness to please.

My name is Patricia Fisher, although I am considering ditching my married name to return to being Patricia Hunter. It doesn't trip so freely from the tongue, but using my married name makes me want to stab something most days. I'll tell you why that is later, but I doubt my tale is much different from that of most divorced, or soon to be divorced, women.

'Is that him, Mrs Fisher?' asked Sam, spotting our quarry before I even noticed someone coming.

Turning my eyes in the direction Sam was casually glancing – he knew better than to stare – I saw the man we expected to see pulling to a stop in a van.

Today was the culmination of months of work. Not that I had performed any of that work. In truth, I only found out about the case a few hours ago. Sam and I are passengers aboard the flagship of Purple

Star Cruise Line. The Aurelia is a magnificent vessel, over a thousand feet from end to end with roughly ten thousand passengers and crew on her at any one time. She and I have some history. It can be measured in months rather than years, but there has been a lot packed into that period.

That I was currently still classed as a passenger was about to change. The same would be true of Sam if his parents, Melissa and Paul could be convinced to let him stay on board as my assistant. I first employed him a few months ago back home in England, but when yesterday I approached the captain of the ship and asked him to create a new position of *Ship's Detective,* I requested that Sam be allowed to stay on too.

Whether the people at the cruise line headquarters agree to all or even any of it is yet to be seen, but they wasted no time in devising a test for me: find out where the missing inventory is going.

A huge ship like the Aurelia must take on and store a vast amount of food and drink, among other things, each time it docks. Given the luxury nature of the ship, high-end, high value items such as lobster, caviar, champagne, to name just three, are served daily. The turnover would make the average person's eyes water and all that falls under the control of a person known as the purser.

Equal in rank to the captain, but not equal in position, the purser controls all the financial aspects of the ship and manages its cargo. I learned today that each kitchen, of which there are many, must manage its own inventory but there are not enough storerooms for each kitchen to have their own and here is where the problem arises.

The inventories do not tally.

The reason I mentioned lobster, caviar, and champagne earlier, is because those are three of the items that have been going missing. It is the latter two which will get the thieves caught.

I stepped back out of view to speak into my radio. 'Does anyone else have eyes on? I want to be one hundred percent certain before I swoop.'

I got silence in reply for a couple of beats, then a crackle as someone pressed the transmit button. 'This is Bhukari. I have eyes on. It's him.'

The radio clicked again as she cleared the airwaves and someone else spoke. 'This is Pippin. I'm on the street still. He hasn't seen me, and I am ten feet away, It's definitely him.'

That was good enough for me. 'Take him.'

I had four members of the ship's security team with me. They would do the taking, not me. I am a fifty-three-year-old woman and though I may be fit and healthy, I strenuously avoid getting into fights with grown men. I leave that sort of thing to trained security officers.

We were in Dublin, where yesterday we revealed the identity of one of the world's biggest criminals, an underworld crime boss calling herself The Godmother. She was in custody now as were other criminals working for her all around the globe. It was breaking news on every news channel in every country, but I had no time to bask in my own glory. Besides, I was just one part of the machine that took her down and would have perished along the way were it not for loyal, amazing, and talented friends.

The ship was due to set sail in just a couple of hours, which was why Sam had been clock watching. We would make it though. All we had to do was make an arrest.

I stepped out from my position behind a wall, intentionally drawing the man's attention. There was a moment where his eyes flicked my way, surprised to see someone his brain told him he recognised, then indecision as he attempted to work out why he knew my face.

To most of the crew I am just a passenger on board the ship, but more and more of them know me as the captain's girlfriend. Captain Alistair Huntley makes a point of promenading around the upper deck and in the public areas with me as a couple. However, it wasn't my status as the captain's other half that held the eyes of the man looking at me. It was the part of his brain that controlled memory and had just told him he was in deep doodoo.

'Hello,' I said, a pleasant smile on my face. 'What's in the van?'

If the van was loaded with goods from the Aurelia's hold, there would be no defence in the world that would help him. 'What's that got to do with you?' the man sneered gruffly. It was a threat, but I could tell his heart wasn't in it. His brain was telling him he was busted, spinning his adrenalin up to high gear so it would be ready for fight or flight.

I was the only person he could see. Not that I was the only person on the street, but in a busy backstreet area of Dublin, everyone else was going about their business, too preoccupied with their own tasks to pay attention to a man making a delivery in a nondescript white van. In contrast to everyone else, I was directly in his field of vision.

'Let's take a look, shall we?' suggested Lieutenant Deepa Bhukari, stepping out from her position across the street where she had been pretending to trade with a man selling wholesale boxes of fruit. The fruit seller was Lieutenant Schneider, a tall, broad-shouldered Austrian.

Deepa's comment made the man's head spin around, taking his eyes off me. Sam stepped out to join me on the pavement and movement from the rear of the van exposed Lieutenant Baker, another member of the ship's security team and one of my close friends. Suddenly the man was surrounded, hemmed in on all sides, but just when we were taking control of the situation and moments away from making an arrest, a wide roller door to my right shot upwards to slam against its stops.

Everyone froze, the loud suddenness of the noise the roller door made drawing everyone's eyes toward what was behind it.

My heart tapped out a staccato as a dozen unpleasant looking men looked out from within.

'What's going on, Freddie?' asked a possible spokesperson in a thick, threatening, but nevertheless delightful Dublin accent. His face bore a look of mild amusement, as if he had taken in the scene before him, deciphered it and decided our presence to be entertaining. 'Friends of yours, are they?' the man asked.

Freddie, an Australian member of crew otherwise known as Rating Third Class Frederick Gumbolt, swallowed hard, before replying. 'No, Oscar. These are not my friends. I don't know who they are,' he lied. His eyes were flitting between me and Sam, and Oscar surrounded by his unpleasant looking colleagues.

They were black-market traders ready to collect a van filled with high value goods from the Aurelia. They operated an illegal business and were used to the violent trappings that went with it. Even a cursory glance would tell a person these men didn't spend a lot of time collecting for charity.

Wanting to nip the situation in the bud and hoping Oscar would see the sense in just letting us take Freddie, I took a step forward. 'Rating Third Class Gumbolt has a van full of stolen goods. We are going to retrieve those goods and take him into custody. We have no interest in you.'

I was letting Oscar know that he could close his roller door and forget about Freddie without needing to worry about his day going south. We are not the police, you see, just a security force from the cruise line. Outside of the dock we have no jurisdiction.

Unfortunately, Oscar was brighter than I wanted him to be. He chuckled at me and wagged a finger, telling me off. 'You're from the ship and that means you have no authority here. You swam away from your little pond, and into my great big ocean. I am king here. But …' he paused for effect, 'since you are gracious enough to offer to leave me alone, I shall extend the same to you. Leave now and I will let you go.'

I shook my head. 'We will be leaving with Rating Third Class Gumbolt and the van.'

Oscar's voice dropped to a low growl; I was beginning to try his patience.' 'It's my van.'

Baker caught my eye as he moved forward. This was a nervous moment. They had us outnumbered greater than two to one and that was if we included Sam and me. They might be armed too whereas we were most definitely not. Baker's face bore an expression that begged me to tread carefully.

Before I could say anything more, Oscar's mood lightened, and he grinned at me. 'Now you see, Mrs …'

'Fisher. Patricia Fisher,' I supplied, hoping he might know the name and sense that he was in more trouble than he originally estimated.

He didn't. 'Mrs Fisher, the goods in that van there belong to me. I have already bought them, isn't that right, Freddie?'

'Yes, Oscar,' replied Freddie, nervously, his eyes still darting about as if looking for a magical escape route from his current situation.

'And I have already sold them on to other persons,' Oscar continued. 'Commerce in action, one might say. Supply and demand. People demand and I do my best to supply them. Now, what do you think it would do to my reputation if I were to let these goods which I have already sold, leave with you?'

He didn't expect an answer; it had been posed as a rhetorical question. But before he could say anything further, I replied, 'Better a dent in your reputation than the alternative.'

We were now in a stand-off. My four security officers, all in plain clothes and without their sidearms for we were far away from the docks, had moved in closer to Freddie. He wasn't going anywhere, but Oscar's men were just a few feet in front of him. Looking poised and dangerous, they were fanned out to the left and right of their boss and their feet were twitching.

Raising a hand to tell his men to hold in place for a few more seconds, Oscar frowned at me. 'What alternative, Mrs Fisher? You have no power here, no authority to arrest anyone. I can have my men beat you and your colleagues to death and dump you from a boat into the Irish Sea tonight. Your ship will sail without you.' My heart was banging so loudly in my chest now, I was beginning to have trouble making out what he was saying. 'Will you make that necessary, Mrs Fisher? Or will you see sense and remove yourself before I release my men?'

I took a step back, my rear foot leaving the pavement as I stepped into the road to gain some distance. 'You intend to take possession of these goods even though you know they are stolen?'

Oscar knew he had won – power of numbers and the threat of violence sufficient to get him what he wanted without the need for actual bloodshed.

'Yes, Mrs Fisher. That is my business.' Oscar flicked the fingers of one hand to send his men forward to the van.

One of them, standing just behind Oscar, had been looking at me for the last minute with a perplexed expression. 'Ere, Oscar, I think I know her,' the man, his neck non-existent as his huge bald head tiered directly into his shoulders, nodded in my direction.

Baker, Bhukari, and the others were all backing away from Rating Third Class Gumbolt and the van as Oscar's men came forward. Freddie still looked nervous – he'd been caught, so while he would satisfy Oscar and get paid, he couldn't return to the ship ever and that left him more than a little stuck.

The man with no neck was bringing up a phone to show Oscar, the screen no doubt displaying a picture of me since there were news articles being run with my name on the headline this morning.

We were out of time, so I lifted the radio to my lips once again. 'Will that do?'

A man's voice cut across the airwaves. 'Yes, Mrs Fisher. Thank you.'

Oscar was halfway through the motion of glancing down at the phone when he heard the first siren. His eyes snapped up to meet mine, wide with panic as Garda police cars entered the street from both ends.

I returned Oscar's gaze, giving him a pinky wave with the hand holding the radio next to my face.

Oscar's men couldn't work out where to go. One moment they were about to unload a van, the next they were trying to work out which direction they could go to flee the Garda. Four cars were screaming along the road from each direction, their sirens blaring and their roof lights strobing.

There was no chance for escape, no place Oscar and his men could run, but that didn't stop them trying. My team were ready for that though.

Schneider, giant lump of man that he is, laid out the scumbag nearest to him with a single piledriver of a punch. Then grabbed the next man and threw him up against the side of the van to leave a head-shaped dent.

Pippin, far smaller in every direction, nevertheless felled another by whipping his legs around to trip him, while Baker and Bhukari demonstrated their own skills in hand-to-hand combat. Oscar's men were probably carrying weapons but none of them were afforded the chance to draw whatever knives or other blunt objects they might have.

Freddie started to move, choosing to run for it as his flight instinct kicked in. His feet stopped so fast he almost toppled when I barked. 'Stay right there, Rating Gumbolt!'

The man with no neck ran for the rear of the building, aiming to escape somehow though I knew the Garda had officers approaching from that direction too. However, Oscar never bothered to move. His eyes were locked on mine as the mayhem ensued around us.

'You're right,' I told him. 'I have no authority outside of the docks.' The Garda police cars screeched to a stop one after the other, the officers inside all piling out to round up Oscar's men. Among them, one man elected to stroll through the chaos, choosing to join me instead of helping his fellow officers.

'Mrs Fisher,' he acknowledged me with a dip of his head.

'Do you know Inspector Meanan?' I asked Oscar.

Oscar just blew out a frustrated breath and looked at the ground disappointed as officers swooped upon him.

Catching the thief was the task handed down by Purple Star's people, but to me that felt like applying a band aid rather than dealing with the root cause. There would be other black marketeers everywhere we went, and perhaps we would get to each of them in turn. However, one call to the local police in Dublin had enabled me to set up a sting operation.

My team had already done the leg work to identify the likely culprit from the crew. Making certain we had the right person took no more than a few hours of observation. Freddie couldn't have done it alone, so there would be further arrests once we were back at the ship. For now, I was enjoying the show as Oscar and his men were loaded into the back of a waiting Garda van.

'That was quite masterful, Mrs Fisher,' Inspector Meanan congratulated me. 'He admitted to handling stolen goods and to distribution. You've saved us weeks of work.'

'It was my pleasure. Thank you for being on hand to rescue us. I'm glad it wasn't necessary.' Things could have gone quite differently had Oscar decided we posed a threat after all.

The inspector needed to go about his business; they had a building to search and prisoners to process. Beginning to move away, he asked, 'You'll be leaving now? Your ship sails soon?'

Baker, Bhukari, and my assistant, Sam Chalk, were in the front seats of the van. Schneider and Pippin were either side of Freddie in the rear of a

Garda police car, all bound for the docks where they would find the Aurelia, return the goods and lock Rating Third Class Gumbolt in the brig.

Moving away myself, I said, 'Soon. I have just enough time for a lunch date.'

The inspector nodded appreciatively, perhaps admiring my use of time or cockiness in organising a date on the assumption this would be done and dusted. 'You have done me a good favour today, Mrs Fisher. If you are ever in the area and feel I can repay it, I would appreciate the opportunity.'

I let him go with a respectful dip of my head for his kind offer. It was generous of him, but I doubted I would ever have reason to make the call.

Lunch Date

Feeling cocky about my day when I left the ship, I had already made a plan to meet my boyfriend, Captain Alistair Huntley, for lunch at one of the best restaurants in Dublin. High on a rooftop overlooking the city, we would have some rare time to ourselves.

One of the cruise line's sleek, black limousines waited for me a short walk from the location of the back street bust. I was already dressed for the occasion in a figure-hugging dress which flared from the waist to end a few inches below my knees. It was sleeveless, which might not sound like the best choice for late autumn in Dublin, but with a winter coat over my top half, I had been warm enough.

In the car, I switched my shoes, losing the flat pumps I opted for in case things went sideways apprehending Freddie. Replacing them with a pair of heels that gave me extra height - needed since Alistair stood over six feet tall.

Traffic was light, and though I was running a little late, it was not until I had thanked the driver and walked into the restaurant that my phone pinged with a message from Alistair to check on me.

He didn't know about the bust. Only that I told him I would meet him at the restaurant. I kissed him lightly on the cheek when the waiter led me to his table and led with, 'Rating Third Class Gumbolt is in the brig. He was the one selling inventory.'

Alistair stared at me with an open mouth for a second before choking out a chuckle of shock. 'Already? Purple Star only asked about that case ...' he checked his watch, 'six hours ago.'

I picked up my water to sip it. 'Shall we have wine?' I asked, then thought better of it. 'I rather fancy trying Guinness. I've never had it before.'

Alistair blinked, distracted by my question but then pulling me back to my previous statement about Freddie. 'Patricia that case has been unresolved for months.'

Signalling the waiter, I said, 'I deserve only a small portion of the credit. Most of the work was already done. Baker and the others are back at the Aurelia now where they will be squeezing Freddie to give up the other people involved. It's really down to the security team that we caught him.' When the waiter approached, I ordered myself a pint of the black stuff, getting one for Alistair too when he nodded an answer to my question. I was going to get to see if it left a foamy white moustache on my upper lip when I took my first sip. I'd seen it do that to a lady in a movie once and the image – a romantic one – had stuck in my head.

While our drinks were being poured and we perused the menus, selecting fresh oysters followed by John Dory fillets on a bed of samphire with a passionfruit glaze, I told him about the Garda and Oscar and how the team did their best to make the cruise line look good.

'You certainly achieved that,' Alistair acknowledged. 'Was the extra effort just to impress Purple Star? Because I'm fairly sure they are going to offer you whatever you want.'

'Do you think so?'

Alistair chuckled again. 'You have made Purple Star really rather famous in the last few months. Not always for the right reasons granted, but none of the negative stuff was your fault. The way I hear it, the marketing people are hanging up their hats because everyone wants to travel with Purple Star. The other cruise lines are trying to work out how they can get some terrorists on board just to add a little excitement.'

As my eyes widened, I said, 'You're joking.'

He gave me a half shrug. 'Probably. But not about them giving you whatever you want. I'm confident they'll give Sam a position too. How will you manage that though? He needs a person to assist him, does he not?'

Our drinks arrived, along with our first course and the conversation died for a minute while the waiter arranged our plates, and we sampled our drinks.

When the waiter withdrew, I said, 'I plan to hire someone.' Sam was capable of looking after himself up to a point. However, he could be easily distracted, and it would not be safe to leave him to manage his own life. I expected the opportunity to be his live-in helper would appeal to a young person since the work required would be minimal and they would get to travel the world.

Lunch was lovely, the two of us left completely alone by everyone which was almost impossible aboard the ship. Alistair's role as captain demanded a lot of his time, time he had always been willing to give before because he had so few distractions. Now there was me, and he was trying to work out how to spend more time in my company.

We chatted back and forth about many subjects, not least of which was my imminent move to join him in the captain's quarters on the bridge. My belongings are currently in the Windsor Suite, the finest suite on the ship, and one intended for royalty if they ever choose to stay. I couldn't remain there now, and my decision to stay on the ship was really a decision to stay with Alistair.

The ship would sail in the next hour, its destination Southampton on the south coast of England. I needed to disembark at that point, heading home to my village in Kent where I would take care of the divorce hanging over my head. During my absence, my things would be transferred to Alistair's cabin and the ship would sail onward to the Mediterranean. I would catch up to it there.

However, when I mentioned going home to sort out my affairs, Alistair said something that jolted me. 'I'm sorry, what was that?' I begged him to repeat himself.

He cleared his mouth. 'I said, I was planning to come with you. I'm curious to see where you live and where you grew up. It's the same place, right?'

I nodded. 'What about the ship?'

Alistair raised an eyebrow. 'You mean who will captain it? I do get holiday, Patricia. I'm not expected to be on the ship every day of the year. They will send in a temporary captain, someone who has risen through the ranks and is vying for a ship of their own. It gives the cruise line the chance to test them out for a few weeks without committing anything.'

'How much holiday do you have saved up?'

'Two months.'

I choked in surprise. 'Two months! I wasn't planning to be home for that long.'

'No doubt. If it pleases you to have me with you, I will accompany you home from Southampton and we can return to the ship as soon as you wish, or as soon as your business at home is concluded.'

My mind was racing now, trying to work things out in my head. Was there any reason at all not to take Alistair home with me? Petty reasons why I should take him, such as letting Angelica Howard-Box see me with a handsome man surfaced and were dismissed – well sort of dismissed; I really wanted that to happen but would never voice it. The divorce was all but a formality. I had paperwork to sign if I chose to do so. Charlie's lawyers had it all worked out and I was yet to even hire a divorce lawyer of my own.

A question occurred to me, 'How much notice do you need to give?'

He shot me a sly grin. 'I booked my time off a week ago.'

The cheeky so and so had guessed I would defeat the Godmother and would then be getting off the ship. I should have been pleased, of course, because his plan had been to give me enough time to come to my senses and let him back into my life. That happened anyway, but with his time off planned, we could spend some time together away from the ship.

I was quite excited by the prospect.

The limousine took us back to the ship where the temporary captain, a fifty-two-year-old American woman called Janice Stubbs, was on board taking control already. A commander by rank, she would wear the rank of captain for the next few weeks. Taking over the role immediately, she would nevertheless be shadowed by Alistair for the next twenty-four hours until we arrived in Southampton.

Alistair had nothing but praise for her, saying more than once it was about time the cruise line gave a woman her own ship. Apparently, Miss Stubbs was the first ever woman to be given the captaincy of a Purple Star cruise liner and would be the first to ever be promoted to captain if her brief tenure proved successful.

The ship was being prepared to set sail once more, the quayside a bustle of human traffic, but while the main entrance was shutting down, we were not the only late arrivals at the royal suites' entrance farther up the ship's hull.

A small van was being unloaded by porters while a tall thin man with wispy grey hair pulled into a long ponytail gave directions. If the set of his face was anything to go by, he was being unpleasant about it. He looked to be in his sixties and was dressed so scruffily, I wanted to question what he could possibly be doing in a royal suite if he wasn't cleaning or robbing it. Of course, I remembered what I looked like when I first boarded the Aurelia and knew I had no room nor reason to comment.

Standing a few yards away from the scruffy man were two young women in their early twenties, his daughters, I assumed, though both looked nothing like him or like each other. In fact, now I was assessing them, they looked like they could be super models.

Waiting close to the awning over the gangplank as porters rushed by her was a woman with a clipboard. She was dressed in a thick parka that looked in need of being replaced, and when she turned her head to speak to one of the porters, I could see she was also around my age and attractive like the young women. She bore no resemblance to them, making me dismiss the assumption she might be the mother to one or both.

Standing close to her was a man mountain. A few years younger, perhaps in his mid-forties, the man had a serious gym obsession. In a winter coat left undone, possibly because it wouldn't go around him, his shape screamed bodybuilder.

'Can you hurry up, Evelyn?' shouted a woman emerging from behind the van. The new arrival wore a flaming red dress that reminded me of a flamenco dancer. Over the top she wore an elegant black coat with big silver buttons, the type designed for fashion rather than function. 'It's cold out here,' she snapped. The woman, whoever she was, was in her late thirties, had beautiful straight, dark brown hair hanging down her back, bright red lipstick, and matching shoes.

Evelyn identified herself as the woman standing by the gangplank by snapping back an answer. 'Wear something sensible then, you daft banana.'

Evelyn didn't actually use the word banana, but a different word that also begins with a B. If it was intended to incite an angry response, it got one.

The woman in the red dress surged forward, but not to get to the woman at the gangplank, she went to the older man with the ponytail. 'August, I'm going to stab her with something if you don't reel her in. Why is she here anyway?'

'Because nothing happens without me organising it!' yelled Evelyn. 'You would run out of clean knickers in a week without me!' I want to say there was an undercurrent of malice between the two women, but it wasn't an undercurrent, hidden from sight and deadly only if you went too close. It was on the surface like a flood, threatening to sweep away all in its path.

'You're not needed!' screamed the younger woman.

As the verbal battle went back and forth, and porters carried what looked like blank canvases onto the ship along with the luggage, Alistair nodded his head toward the man with the ponytail, 'That's August Skies.'

'August Skies?' I repeated. I'd never heard of him though Alistair said it as if it were a household name.

Alistair explained, 'He's a famous artist. The cruise line has commissioned him to paint a series of pieces of the Aurelia as she cruises around the world. He's on board for several months. Actually, he and his entourage are staying in the suite next to yours.'

I curled my lip. 'If he's famous, can I also assume he is rich? Why's he so scruffy?'

'Ah,' said Alistair. 'Well, that's one of his peculiarities. He eschews money. His works could fetch millions, but he refuses to sell them. He will only accept commissions, such as the one Purple Star have engaged him for, if there is something of value that he wants which isn't money. In this case, it is a long stay in a suite and a trip around the world.'

'For him and his … are they his daughters? I asked.

The chauffeur came around to Alistair's door and pulled it open. A slight drizzle had settled in, damping the quayside and the air outside. Alistair slid across the seat to get out and reached back to take my hand. 'I think you'll find they are his models. He paints a lot of nudes.'

I hitched an eyebrow. 'And that's what Purple Star wants?'

The captain of the ship laughed this time. 'No, I believe they want paintings of the ship set against majestic backdrops. He could do it all from his studio from photographs, but … well, I take you back to the point about not taking money and wanting something of value instead. I believe the … ah, young ladies, are muses of some sort.'

My other eyebrow shot to join the first. So far as I was aware, the term muse was generally a polite substitute for person with whom said artist is having relations. 'Is he married to one of the older women?'

Alistair pulled me from the car and into his arms with enough force to make sure I fell against him. Once I was off-balance, he dipped me and kissed me on the lips. 'Do you think this would make a good painting?' he asked with a wink when he broke the kiss.

I slapped his arm. 'Let me up, Alistair. You're so embarrassing.' My cheeks flushed as the few people still on the quayside all looked our way.

Heading to the royal suites entrance where we would have to go around the argument still raging there, Alistair said, 'To answer your question: both.'

Twisted Relationships

Back in my suite for what was to be the last time, I found Barbie relaxing on a couch with three miniature dachshunds. All three looked my way and would have known someone was coming in because my butler, Jermaine, had crossed the room to get to the door.

Normally, the dogs would leap from the couch to fly at the door when someone came in but must have decided they were just too comfortable to risk getting up.

Barbie lifted her head and waved. 'Hi, Patty.'

Barbie is a size zero, twenty-two-year-old perfect Californian blonde. She is also a gym instructor on board the ship and one of my very best friends. Currently, she is living in one of the many bedrooms in the palatial Windsor Suite, but like me, is soon to move out. In her case, she is going to join her boyfriend, the newest doctor to join the crew.

Jermaine, my butler, is a Jamaican man with a fake Downton Abbey accent. At six feet four inches tall, he is imposing, but there is no sense of danger from him until he decides it is time for action. At that point, he transforms into a muscular ninja with the skills to match. He is my bodyguard when I need him to be, and I couldn't hope to count the number of times he has saved my life since I met him.

I love him as much as any woman can love a man while maintaining a platonic relationship.

He took my coat and brushed it to remove the few spots of rain on the shoulders before placing it on a hanger in the closet by the main entrance door.

Coming into the suite, I told Barbie and Jermaine about Freddie Gumbolt, the stolen goods, and the Garda. They already knew I was involved in the case and about my plan to take a role on board the ship as its official detective.

As I crossed the room to see the dogs, Barbie shifted Smokey, the little boy dachshund, onto the carpet. The girls, Anna and Georgie jumped down after him, all three performing a routine of stretches – which on a dog already too long to be natural is quite a sight. I had recently come to be looking after Smokey when it was discovered he had been snatched by the Godmother to give her something in common with me.

'I found his owner,' Barbie announced, lithely rising to her feet, and doing her own stretches.

The news ought to have come as no surprise; Barbie is no slouch. It was her work, together with Hideki, Jermaine, and others, that resulted in the Godmother losing in her bid to kill us all. Barbie had the genius idea that unravelled the world's largest organised crime syndicate, and it seemed woefully unfair that I was the one getting all the recognition.

'How?' I asked, curious to hear how she had tracked down the dog's owner in such a short space of time with so little to go on.

'I phoned a few veterinarian surgeries in the general area.' Verity had been good enough to reveal that she had taken the dog from outside a post office in Longwell Green. 'I was lucky enough to find someone who knew the dog on my fifth call.'

I scooped Smokey, much to the disappointment of the other two dogs and held him aloft while he tried to lick my nose. 'We're going to take you home, little man. Does that sound good?' Turning my attention to Barbie, I asked, 'Did you get to speak to the owner?'

'Yes. The staff at the vet's wouldn't give me the number, of course, but were good enough to take mine and pass it on. He belongs to Sarah Flett. She sounded young on the phone ...' Barbie paused for thought. 'She had a very different accent to you ... or anyone else I ever heard from England.'

'Ah, yes. That's the West Country,' I chuckled. 'The Bristol area, in fact. Regional accents across England are magnificent.'

Barbie wiggled her eyebrows in thought. 'Anyway, she burst into tears when I described Smokey and his collar. Then I told her where he is and had to explain that her little dog had been on something of an adventure. She's planning to meet us at Southampton tomorrow.'

I would be sad to see the little dog go. I suspected my own dogs would too. The three of them had taken to sleeping like a bag of snakes, all twisted around on top of one another, so it was hard to work out where one dog ended and the next started sometimes.

Thinking about Southampton led me nicely to another item of news, so I told her and Jermaine about Alistair's plan to accompany me back to the house in Kent.

'That will be fun, Patty,' said Barbie. 'We are all going.'

Jermaine and Barbie both had belongings at the house in Kent which they hadn't brought with them when we fled to the ship to avoid the Godmother's assassins. They wouldn't collect them all – we were not moving out, but our return to the Aurelia was supposed to be a temporary thing and now it was becoming indefinite.

Indefinite. It was a word that scared me more than a little. I could not picture myself staying on board forever. Equally, I couldn't happily picture me leaving yet either. The two things were opposites – I couldn't do both, so I was procrastinating: putting the decision off. No doubt I would be forced to decide at some point, but that wasn't now.

'Tea, madam?' asked Jermaine.

I checked the clock on the wall in the kitchen, and told myself with a sigh, that it was a little early for gin. 'Yes, please, Jermaine sweetie.'

'What time are we meeting the others?' asked Barbie, following Jermaine and me into the kitchen area of the suite.

We had a plan to meet our friends for dinner. It was our last night on board together and our last chance for a get-together as a group. I had no idea when I might see some of them again for by tomorrow night, the party from Zangrabar would be returning there. Lady Mary Bostihill Swank was off to join her husband on a book-signing tour for his new thriller and Mike Atwell would return to his job as a detective sergeant in the Kent police – he was undecided about taking over the daily management of my private investigations business, but even if he took me up on my offer, he would still need to give notice and serve a period before he could do something else.

Sam Chalk was to stay with me, I hoped, his parents were yet to make a final decision though I believed they would choose to give him the fullest life he could achieve and that wasn't going to happen in a quiet village in Kent. His parents had jobs to return to, so either way they were leaving our company.

While Jermaine went about his tea-making ritual and I petted Smokey on my lap at the breakfast bar, I thought to ask my friends if they had heard of August Skies.

'The artist?' questioned Jermaine, surprising me. 'He's really quite famous. Mostly for his refusal to sell his art and make a fortune, but also for his twisted relationships.'

Barbie hitched an eyebrow. 'Twisted?'

'He has a small harem, it would seem,' I advised her and then between us, Jermaine and I filled her in on the young models, wife and ex-wife he travelled with. According to Jermaine – which Barbie quickly Googled to confirm – he acted much like a playboy, forging sexual relationships with women openly and with his wife's blessing. He left his first wife when she demanded he stop it, marrying one of the other women in his life only months later.

Once my tea was finished, I slipped from my stool; it was time to take the dogs for a walk. The Aurelia is a big ship with lots of deck to wander if one chooses to do so. Having announced my intention, Barbie bounded away to her room. 'I'll come with you,' she called. 'I just need a coat and gloves.'

Jermaine took the dogs to the door. Or rather, he went, and they scurried after him, keen to go wherever it was the humans were offering to take them. He fitted their collars and leads and waited until Barbie and I were ready.

With warm outer layers added, we set off, turning right outside the door to head for the nearest exit to the deck and the cool Irish air. No more than ten yards later, we heard the shouting.

It was coming through the door of the next suite along – the one where August Skies was now resident.

'Why am I always waiting for her, August!' the question was asked at maximum volume, the tone suggesting the words might have a piece of flying crockery behind them to add emphasis.

It wasn't August who replied, but the raised voice of a young woman who we heard next. 'Why is she such a cow?'

Before the first woman could respond, a man's voice replied in a bored tone, 'It's all in your mind, Evelyn. Niamh does not have any kind of agenda against you. Do you, Niamh?'

Prompted by his question, a voice replied, 'Not one I'll admit to.' The voice belonged to the woman in the red dress, I judged, who I now knew to be his wife, Niamh. Of course, being Irish, Niamh is pronounced Neave despite how it is written. Her response carried amused disdain. She was telling anyone who wanted to hear that she didn't care about Evelyn's opinion and was going to do whatever she wanted regardless of its impact on her husband's ex-wife.

Ashamedly, Barbie and I were paused in the passageway outside their suite, listening to hear what would be said next.

Growling, Evelyn said, 'You're so blind, Niamh. Do you really think he will treat you any differently than me? All the attention he lavishes on Vanessa, do you think it is coincidence that you are the same age I was when he exchanged me for you? When he pushes you out, you won't get to be his manager, he'll have no purpose for you at all.'

'He won't leave me like he did you,' snapped Niamh.

Evelyn chortled at her opponent's reply. 'You're a fool, Niamh. He will leave you with nothing, just like he did me. If it isn't Vanessa, it will be Scarlet he leaves you for. Or the next woman who comes along. You're losing your looks … the vibrancy of youth, just like I did. My money is on Vanessa.'

'Both of you stop it, please.' It was the first time August had spoken. 'The circumstances now are completely different, Evelyn. I still love you … in a different way to Niamh. I am glad to have you managing my life. No one knows my artistic requirements better than you.'

'Really?' Snapped Niamh. 'You love her.'

August tried to defend his statement. 'My feelings for Evelyn are different to how I feel about you.' He sounded more annoyed than anything. The two quarrelling women were distracting him from whatever else he wanted to do.

'And you're not about to leave me for Vanessa?' Niamh demanded he make a statement to that effect.'

Evelyn chuckled at the doubt she had sown.

August said. 'I will not be cornered on such subjects, Niamh. I simply will not.'

Barbie and I were exchanging a glance and making awkward faces at each other when we heard the sound of feet stomping in our direction. We both tried to get out of the way since we were right outside the door, but while Barbie aimed herself the way we had been going, I tried to escape to the safety of my own suite again.

Inevitably, I bumped into Barbie, bounced off, caught my foot in the dog leads because the dogs were confused about which way we wanted them to go, and fell against the door.

Just as it opened.

With a squeal of panic, I fell backward through the door, colliding with Niamh, still in her gorgeous red dress as she tried to storm out.

Shocking her, she too screamed, and the dogs barked at the sudden presence of an additional person, twelve tiny feet running forward to protect their pack from whoever it was but running over me in the process of trying to get there.

In the space of a heartbeat, I was on the deck, on my back, half in and half out of August Skies' cabin, with dachshund leads wrapped around me like I was caught inside some kind of oversized cat's cradle.

Barbie sniggered, which didn't help one bit. I shot her a mean look and thrust out an arm so she could haul me back to my feet. I risked a glance inside the suite. From my position, I could see through the lobby and into the main living area. August was standing with his back to the door, a smock covering his clothes to protect them because he was painting. Evelyn, her face red and angry, was looking my way, making me avert my eyes, but not before I spotted the two women, one of whom was posing topless, but facing away, while the artist caught her image on canvas. The last person I saw was the butler; easy to identify because he wore the same outfit as Jermaine.

'Sorry about that,' I apologised to the world in general once I was the right way up once more.

Niamh, standing just inside the door to the suite, unable to exit because we were still blocking her path was visibly fuming, her face red with rage. 'That's perfectly all right,' she hissed. 'I'm sure listening at doors is perfectly normal for some people.'

Abruptly, she shoved by me, knocking my shoulder as she barged through a gap that wasn't there. Two paces later, and still in sight of the three people left inside the suite, she stopped and turned to face them.

'I'm going to find a spa, August. That's included in our package, right? Lord knows there's no money to go to one at home.' She all but spat the words, filling them with venom and menace, and then she was gone, stomping along the passageway.

I was speechless; caught in an ugly feud and unable to work out which way I should look. Barbie came to my rescue, grabbing my arm to tug me forward and away from the suite. The dogs started trotting again, keen to get outside. Just as we were going through the door onto the deck, the door to the suite slammed shut.

Mercifully, the rest of our walk went without incident and the dogs got to scurry about, racing here and there off their leads in a confusing game of chase where they all seemed to be trying to chase each other while simultaneously running away.

Barbie used her key card to swipe the door open, the dogs trotting through the door ahead of us. Jermaine appeared in the next second as if he had been waiting just outside the suite's lobby for us the whole time.

As was his practice, he took the dog leads, shucked their collars and led them through to the kitchen for it was doggy dinner time now and the three hounds knew it. I made it a habit of mine to feed them their meals, letting Jermaine fill in if for some reason I could not be there.

Three bowls of dog chow were filled from three small pouches of gourmet dog food, if such a thing can be believed to exist. Regardless of my thoughts on the matter, the dachshunds made the food disappear in seconds, attacking it as though a starting gun had been fired and first to finish won a prize of some kind.

When they were done licking the top layer of enamel from their bowls, I collected them for Jermaine to place in the dishwasher and gratefully accepted the balloon glass of gin and tonic he held in his left hand.

In an hour he and I, together with Barbie, were joining an ensemble cast of friends for one last meal. I was sad that we would not see some of those attending for some time – it was possible we might never see them again – but filled with happiness that I had such good friends in the first place.

Alistair was coming too, for he had been a pivotal member of the team that took down the Godmother and her Alliance of Families. I carried my glass of gin to my bedroom, ran a bath and emerged an hour later to find Barbie, her boyfriend Hideki, and Jermaine waiting for me. Hideki, a man we met driving a taxi in Tokyo to pay his medical school tuition fees, looked handsome in a dark blue suit over an auburn shirt. He was shorter than Barbie, but unlike many men who get weird about such things, he didn't seem to care.

For once, Jermaine was dressed neither as a butler nor as Steed from the TV series *The Avengers*. He wore a fitted grey wool suit that made him appear tall and regal.

Barbie and Hideki were linked with her left hand resting in the crook of his right elbow. Jermaine offered me the same and we all left the suite to meet our friends for dinner.

Along the way, we ran into Alistair. Also dressed in a natty suit, he looked devilishly handsome and had been rushing to get to my suite to collect me. The crazy man even had a corsage.

Jermaine slipped my arm from his, handing me off to the captain with a dip of his head.

In a reserved section of the upper deck restaurant which sat at the front of the ship with panoramic views across the ocean along both sides, we found our friends already there and waiting for us. Rick, a retired detective from Hawaii, was doing his best to shock Lady Mary Bostihill-Swank by spewing his entire repertoire of dirty jokes.

It wasn't going too well for him because the titled British Lady, distantly related to the Queen somewhere in her bloodline, gave as good as she got. We heard Rick finish a joke as we came near and got to listen to Lady Mary fire one back.

I won't repeat it but let's just say it was all to do with three servicemen, their wives on their wedding nights and some brown toast for breakfast the next morning.

Seeing that the final guests had arrived, the Maître D' tinkled a little bell and called us to the table. It wasn't really a formal affair but was set out like one with a long table to seat all thirteen of us. It would have been nice to have the security officers with us as well, but they were working, and we were too short on time to balance our plans with their schedule since all my friends were leaving the next day.

Conversation ranged back and forth, small pockets discussing different subjects. There was much speculation about how much attention I might have drawn to myself. There had already been calls for me to speak to the press from more than a dozen nations. I was not inclined to voice any opinion, convinced I would be misquoted or perhaps correctly quoted saying something stupid.

The first course of giant Dublin Bay langoustines came and went, whetting my appetite for the steak course which followed. However, just after it arrived, dinner was interrupted by the arrival of Lieutenant Bhukari.

I saw her weaving her way through the crowded upper deck restaurant. That she wanted me specifically was clear when she locked eyes and shot me a quick apologetic grimace. Alistair spotted that I was no longer paying attention to what he had been saying and tracked my eyes to find his crewmember heading my way.

I got a feeling I wasn't going to like finding out why she needed me.

'Mrs Fisher,' she whispered, arriving by my right elbow and dropping into a crouch so her head was next to mine. 'Sorry for disturbing your dinner.'

Alistair leaned around the back of my chair so he could hear what she was saying. 'No need for apologies, Lieutenant. Just spit it out.'

'There's been a suicide, sir,' Deepa replied, answering her captain rather than talking to me. 'It's passenger Vanessa Morton, sir. She's staying in the Prestwick Suite, sir.'

I swore inside my head. Her name was one of those I overheard earlier: she was one of August Skies' muses. My eyes closed when I chose to picture her in my head. I knew nothing about the woman, save for her current employment, if such a term applied, and a suspicion that she was involved in a love triangle that might be more of a square or a polygon.

Conversation around the table had already ground to a halt when I reopened my eyes.

'Problem?' asked Rick, voicing the question everyone wanted an answer to.

I gave a half shrug, dabbing my lips with a napkin as I prepared to abandon my meal. 'A body,' I replied at a volume unlikely to be heard by people at the tables around us. 'A suicide,' I added before anyone could ask.

Lieutenant Bhukari came out of her crouch, straightening up once more. 'Lieutenant Baker is there now, Mrs Fisher.' Her simple sentence was nothing of the sort, it was a request that I accompany her back to the woman's cabin. There would be no need for the security team to be involved in a suicide, save for the effort of dealing with the body and making sure the medical team had free and easy access. That Deepa wanted me to know Lieutenant Baker was there meant something was amiss.

When I rose from my seat, Alistair, and then everyone else also stood up.

'Is this a new case, Mrs Fisher?' asked Sam. He was sitting opposite me, nestled in next to his mum on one side and Barbie, who'd taken a natural shine to his easy-going outlook, on the other.

I bit my lip. 'I don't think so, Sam,' I replied, wondering if I was lying because I was already doubting the verdict of suicide given all that I'd heard earlier. 'Please, everyone, carry on with your meals. I will attempt to return shortly.'

Rick tore off the napkin he had stuffed into his collar. 'Nuts to that, Patricia. We operate best as a team.'

I had to love his enthusiasm and attitude, but said, 'I don't think we can arrive mobhanded.' Using my eyes, I indicated just how many of us there were around the table. 'I'll be with Deepa and Martin. Many more than that and we just won't fit.'

Suicide

The passageway leading to Vanessa Morton's cabin was blocked by more members of the security team. Deepa and I passed through them, moving along the passageway in silence while my brain whirled. I have a natural inclination to work things out in my head and often skip over the part where I gather anything resembling evidence. I wanted to assume the suicide was nothing of the sort, but other than a sneaking suspicion, I had no reason to.

I asked Deepa, 'Is Martin suspicious?' I used Lieutenant Baker's first name since I was talking to his fiancée.

'Of the cause of death?' she sought clarity, then wobbled her head as if unsure how to answer. 'It looks very much like she cut her wrists and then drowned in the bath,' To me it seemed as though there was something she wasn't saying. 'There is no sign of a struggle, no bruising on her body, but it also looks like she had taken something.'

'Drugs?'

She nodded. 'It looks that way.'

'If it's a suicide, why am I being involved?' I wanted to know.

Deepa sucked in a breath through her lips. 'Because we want to be sure, Mrs Fisher.'

It was a more honest answer than I expected, and I let it sink in without reply as we went through the door and into the Prestwick Suite. The first thing that struck me was a background smell of paint. It didn't dominate everything, but it was quite unmistakeable. There was something else too, something astringent; turpentine or whatever modern paint thinners were made from.

Seeing my face, Deepa said, 'I know. It gets less noticeable once you have been in here a few minutes.'

I was just going to have to put up with it like everyone else.

There were a dozen people inside. Two medics with a gurney waited patiently to one side for the body to be cleared for release. Two members of the security team stood either side of one room, telling me that the body would be found in there. Also present, I could see August Skies, but he wasn't mourning as one might expect at such a time.

He was painting.

His suite was more or less a mirror image of mine next door, but where the furniture in my living area was tastefully arranged to create different areas, his had been shoved out of the way to create a studio.

On the carpet were cotton sheets speckled with paint. They looked to be new – employed specifically for this purpose. Just off the carpet, in the tiled area of the kitchen, his surviving muse, with tears streaming down her cheeks, sat posing for the artist. A few feet behind her, drinking what looked like neat whiskey was August's current wife, Niamh.

That I mentally labelled her as his current wife said a lot about how I viewed their relationship.

'That's beautiful Scarlet,' cooed August encouragingly. 'Your pain is magnificent.'

'Why, August? Why do you have to paint me now?'

He glanced quickly at his model once more, noting something before swiftly applying a few more lines to the canvas. 'Because the rawness of your emotion cannot be faked, Scarlet. The agony you feel now will come through on the canvas and it will be a masterpiece, my dear.' His tone was calm but distracted – his work was too engrossing for him to give her more than a cursory reply.

'I can't do this,' she snivelled.

The scene made me uncomfortable. Scarlet was deeply upset by her friend's apparent suicide. It was a natural emotion, yet August wanted to harness it and that felt barbaric. Around the room, no one was speaking, and this was why; they were all equally horrified and enraptured at the same time.

Maybe the artist was right. Maybe this was powerful stuff that he was capturing, and it would be his greatest work ever. It still made me sick to my stomach to watch and I wasn't going to stay quiet.

'Hey,' I called. Everyone looked at me, including Scarlet, but not August who snuck another quick glance at his tearful model and added a splash of colour to the painting now taking shape before him. 'Hey,' I repeated a little louder. 'I think you ought to put the brush down and take a break, don't you agree?'

August snuck another glance around the side of his canvas at Scarlet. As he applied the next brush stroke, he said, 'Whoever is speaking should leave my cabin now. You are not welcome.' Other than speaking, he showed no sign that he was even aware there were other people in the room.

'Please,' cried Scarlet. 'I want to stop.'

'Scarlet, you have never been more beautiful,' August insisted. It was a twisted, ugly thing to say.

Scarlet dropped her head as spasms shook her shoulders.

Now angry, I marched across the room intending to snatch the brush from his hand. He jumped from his chair to face me before I could get there, and he looked mad. 'How dare you interrupt me?' He looked over my head, easy since he was most of a foot taller than me. 'You there. You're part of the ship's security team, aren't you? Escort this woman from my suite right now.' His demand was aimed at Deepa who was now on the spot and unsure how to respond.

I saved her from having to do so. 'She cannot do that, Mr Skies. I am here to investigate Vanessa's death.'

The artist looked down his nose at me, taking me in for the first time. 'Why? Who are you?'

'She's Patricia Fisher,' slurred his wife from the breakfast bar in the kitchen. 'She's in all the papers, August. She's more famous than you are.'

The last comment made him narrow his eyes – he didn't like that one bit.

Now that the attention was off her, Scarlet made up her own mind. She had been posed on one of the breakfast barstools which had been set in a clear area of the room. Perched on top of it, she looked as if the floor around her were lava and the stool was her only refuge. Now she fled to her room, vanishing through a bedroom door in a fresh fit of tears.

August jerked his head around to see her back disappear from sight and then swung his eyes back to face me. I felt a little itch at the back of my head. Was I staring at a killer?

He was about to say something, but I got in first. 'You do not appear to be upset about the death of your muse. Why is that?'

His eyes narrowed farther. 'We are nothing more than specks in this world, Mrs Fisher. As individuals we have almost no effect on the planet, yet as a species we are destroying it. Vanessa's death is tragic, but ultimately insignificant. There is no reason to be upset by the passing of a person who added nothing to the world and takes nothing with her.'

His words were cruel and unpleasant, which was exactly what I took the man to be. That he could paint failed to impress me. I sucked in a slow breath through my nose and let it go again. 'Very well.'

He nodded, turning back to his canvas to continue painting even though his model was no longer posing for him. Her face and hair were mostly complete, leaving the background detail to fill in so perhaps he no longer needed her. Whatever the case, it was another demonstration of his rudeness.

It was all quite twisted, a word which kept occurring to me when I thought of the artist and his small entourage. Swivelling on one heel to look at Lieutenant Bhukari, I asked, 'Have we accounted for the whereabouts of all members of the Skies' party?'

Lieutenant Bhukari said, 'Not yet. We had to fetch Mrs Skies … that's Mrs Niamh Skies, I should make clear, from the upper deck spa.' Deepa paused to fish out her tablet to read from notes she'd taken. 'She arrived just after four and was still in there at seven when we found her. That's been verified with the crew working there. Mr Skies says he was painting the victim until five.' I glanced down at a canvas stacked against the wall. It was unfinished but clearly using the attractive Vanessa as a focal point. 'He then left her here to go for what he called an inspirational walk around the deck. She was going for a bath according to him. Scarlet O'Reilly was in her room sleeping the whole time.'

'What about the ex-wife, Evelyn?' I wanted to know.

'Schneider went to look for her and ...' she checked her notes, 'Mr Eoin Planchet. He took Pippin and Kumar with him. I'm sure we'll get a report back from them soon.'

I still wasn't sure why I was involved. My head was filling with questions, but I had been ignoring the voices coming from the victim's room since I arrived, and it was time to see the scene for myself. Putting August, talented artist but awful person, to one side for now, I left the suite's main living area to join whoever was in the bathroom.

Lieutenant Baker heard me coming. Stepping back into the bedroom from the attached private bathroom, he said, 'They're just about to take her from the water. Do you want to see?'

I choked out a sad laugh. 'No, Martin, I do not want to see, but I suppose I have to.' Quite how my life has shifted so that I see so many dead bodies, I have no idea. Or rather, I have a clear idea, but still cannot believe it.

The elegant rolltop bath was positioned in the centre of the bathroom. Vanessa was still in the position she was when they first came in, Martin assured me.

'Who found her?' I asked.

'The other woman,' he replied. 'Scarlet O'Reilly.'

No wonder she was so upset. I addressed Dr David Davis, the ship's senior physician, 'Cause of death?'

He sucked a little air between his teeth. 'I'll need to perform an autopsy to be sure, but she cut both her wrists and bled out. Whether she lost consciousness and slipped beneath the surface to drown before the loss of blood killed her will make little difference to the end verdict, but it was one or the other. The former of course caused the latter.'

'You think it was suicide?' I asked, hitting him with a direct and difficult question.

He sucked some more air. Lieutenant Baker moved to stand beside him, both men staring down at the naked form in the red bathwater. Some blood had dripped over the left side to make a small pool on the floor, but other than that, there was no mess.

'There is no sign of struggle,' Lieutenant Baker commented.

I agreed with him. 'No sign at all. Is there a suicide note?'

Lieutenant Baker shook his head. 'Not yet.'

Dr David dismissed our conversation. 'Bruising may yet appear. Again, I need to perform an autopsy before I can give you any worthwhile information.' He knew I was waiting for him to say more. 'On the face of it, though, I see no reason to believe there was a third party involved.'

I pursed my lips and nodded. 'Lieutenant Baker,' saying his name brought his head and eyes around to look at me. 'Why was I summoned?'

He cringed a little, pulling a face that was part apology and part embarrassment. 'A hunch,' he said. 'We're at sea, you are on board, and there's a body.' His cheeks burned bright red. 'Stands to reason that it's a murder, doesn't it?'

I felt like throwing something at him. 'That's the basis of your hunch? I'm on board so any bodies that show up have to be murder victims.'

I got the apologetic face again. 'Wellllll …'

I waved him into silence and paid closer attention to the room, the victim, and the evidence around me. Next to the bath, sitting on the tile, was an ice bucket with an upended bottle of champagne in it. We would need an autopsy to determine if Vanessa drank it all, so too for the drugs which I could see in a zip-top bag on the bathroom counter. She'd brought them with her and was possibly a regular, if casual, user.

When I last saw her on the quayside, she was youthful and vibrant, healthy looking and full of life. Now she was just an empty shell. I felt bile rising in my throat and looked away. The security team would deal with the physical evidence and the medical team, which now included Barbie's boyfriend Hideki, would determine the true cause of death. However, whether drowning or blood loss, it still looked like suicide and only an itch at the back of my head told me otherwise.

Pondering whether I should head back to dinner and pick this up later if there was any reason to, a shout from the suite's main living area made me jump.

Early Clue

The shout came from August Skies, that much I knew without having to look, but since I was here and wanted a reason to leave the bathroom with the awful body in it, I turned on my heel to see what was angering the artist.

I loved listening to his Irish lilt, I have always found it to be a delightful accent to hear, but boy did he know a lot of curse words. He was stringing them together now, somehow making them sound poetic to my ears with his accent.

Coming back into the living area, which was now his studio, I saw he was waving around a small plastic device. Roughly twice the size of a mobile phone in width and thickness, it was clear there was something wrong with it. I tried to follow his ranting, which was being aimed at anyone in sight.

'Who the expletive took the expletive thing? I will expletive them when I expletive find out who they expletive are. What the expletive expletive expletive could they possibly expletive need it expletive for? I am going to expletive them right in their expletive with my big hairy expletive.' Trust me when I say you don't want the uncensored version.

His wife, Niamh, slid off the breakfast bar stool to calm him down, but wobbled drunkenly when her feet hit the deck. She put an arm out to steady herself, grabbing the kitchen counter for support. Once balanced she took short steps to get to August.

He wasn't staying put though. The device got thrown at an armchair where I could finally see what it was: a blood sugar monitor; the type diabetics use to keep track of their insulin needs. The screen was blank and now I got what was upsetting him. The battery compartment was off, the lid for it presumably still in his hand for the battery itself was missing.

Someone had taken it out to be used elsewhere and he had a right to feel a little miffed. I wasn't sure all the swearing was necessary, but I would have felt a little aggrieved too had it been my very necessary medical device.

Niamh picked the device up and looked to be muttering and shaking her head. Her cheeks were red, and I guess she was the guilty party. Perhaps she had planned to replace it, but the task slipped her mind.

August returned from the bedroom, still swearing, snatched the device from his wife's hands quite rudely and finally lapsed into silence. The device beeped, he used it, and then he went back to his painting.

From where I was standing, just outside of Vanessa's bedroom, I could see in through the door to the open bathroom door and the activity inside. I drifted back to stand in the doorway looking in at an oblique angle so I didn't have to look at Vanessa.

Lieutenant Baker was taking a sample of the bathwater to be analysed, ruling out the possibility that there was something in it that induced unconsciousness. I thought it improbable that her wrists had been cut by someone else but had to acknowledge that it wasn't impossible.

'Deepa said she had taken something,' I prompted as the body was taken from the bathwater as gracefully as the medics could manage.

Lieutenant Baker inclined his head toward the sink and mirror across the room. Vanessa hadn't been on board for very long but long enough to unpack her toiletries. Various bottles and things were laid out haphazardly to the left side of the sink, and to the right, a small black bag about the size of a coffee mug. In it were pills inside a small plastic bag. A small evidence tag was positioned next to it for recording where it was found.

'I'll have them analysed as well,' he promised, 'but I think it likely they are oxycodone, more frequently called oxy.'

I knew what it was but other than being able to say it was a highly addictive painkiller, I couldn't say much about it at all. She got them past the security guards in her luggage or about her person and died with them in her system. Question is, how many did she take? Was it a deliberate dose to eliminate the pain of what she was doing, or had she not taken any at all? The autopsy would show one way or another.

All in all, we had a suicide and there was no need for my involvement.

Baker's radio crackled. 'Baker this is Schneider, over.' The Austrian accent was unmistakable. No one ever mentioned it, but when he spoke English, he sounded a lot like a well-known Austrian bodybuilder who made a career as an action movie star in Hollywood. That he was tall and muscular just added to the comparison.

Baker, still watching the proceedings with morbid interest, tilted his head to the left and reached up to click the button on his radio where it was mounted on his lapel. 'Baker,' he replied, his eyes never leaving the terrible sight of Vanessa's body.

'We're on our way to the brig,' Schneider advised, the news grabbing not just my attention but that of everyone else in the room as well. 'It looks like she did it.'

Baker's eyebrows pinched together as he leaned down to his radio again. 'Say again, over.'

Schneider's voice came loud and clear. 'We have compelling evidence that suggests Evelyn Skies killed the victim. This wasn't a suicide.'

His expression unchanged, Baker said, 'Hold off on the interview. We'll meet you there.' He didn't expand on who the 'we' in that sentence was, but I was going to insinuate myself anyway. Purple Star hadn't employed me yet, but I'd been doing this for free since I came on board. Now that I was going to be the ship's detective, it felt right that I took the lead.

The body was zipped into a black body bag – necessary so they could transport it through the ship without disturbing the passengers. They would take the least travelled route to avoid passengers, but every time the ship stopped, new passengers got on and they were wont to wander, exploring their new surroundings.

'We need to interview August Skies and his wife and Scarlet,' Lieutenant Baker said as if compiling a list. 'The ex-wife's boyfriend too, I guess.'

'Not if the ex-wife confesses,' I pointed out. There was a dark, vengeful part of me that wanted to grill August Skies, but being a pig wasn't a crime and (so far) I had no reason to suspect he was guilty of anything other than being a pig.

The news about the ex-wife, Evelyn threw me off balance a little. I had seen her exchanging insults with her ex-husband's current wife, but what did that have to do with Vanessa? Was this suicide or murder? If it was murder, why would Evelyn want the young woman dead?

Catching myself drawing conclusions before seeing any evidence, I cleared my mind. The death might yet prove to be suicide. If it was murder, then the killer was clever and that could make them dangerous. Whatever the case, I needed to speak with August's ex-wife and that was to be my next order of business.

The paint thinner smell lingered, not enough to make me lightheaded, but sufficient to make me want to leave the suite. Back out in the suite's main living area, August continued to paint, unaffected by the death of his muse and unconcerned about the drama around him. I watched him for more than a minute as the medics silently wheeled Vanessa's body through the suite and out the door.

Niamh crossed the room to see the body leave, a sickened look on her face. She'd had too much to drink by my judgement and would be heading for bed shortly. Scarlet did not appear, nor did I hear her in her room as her friend's body was taken away.

It was August though, who I felt compelled to watch. He painted with skill, adding subtle lines here and there in a display of talent I could never imagine possessing. In my head I noted that some people are just born with an ability others do not have and he was one of the lucky ones who found his.

It could be argued that I was lucky too, though the ability to solve a murder wasn't a skill I would have lined up to get. What struck me as I watched him was how disconnected he seemed from the events of the day. Was I witness to a killer so cold-blooded he felt no remorse or pity, or was this a display of an artist's ability to be in the moment? Was he one with the painting, and thus mentally and emotionally shut off from the death of a young woman he knew intimately?

If I had ten seconds to solve the case and had to pick one person as the likely murderer, assuming it was indeed murder and not suicide, then it would have to be him. The back of my skull itched again as I stared at him working, but the brig beckoned so I turned on my heel and left his suite.

Compelling Evidence

Lieutenant Schneider referred to the evidence against Mrs Skies as compelling. That she was still Mrs Skies made my mental referencing difficult, so I chose to label her as Evelyn the Ex instead. I was keen to see what Schneider had against her since clearly he felt it was enough to take her into custody on the spot.

I wasn't a fan of the brig. I'd been incarcerated there and though it was only briefly, the experience stuck in my head so on my way there now, my insides felt jangly and nervous. Negative emotions were rising to make me feel out of sorts. I bit them down, though not as completely or convincingly as I hoped.

'Everything all right, Mrs Fisher?' asked Lieutenant Baker in the elevator as we travelled down through the ship. The brig is located in the bowels of the Aurelia, below the passenger decks where problems can be kept well away from the passengers paying a small fortune to enjoy their time at sea.

I huffed and let my shoulders slump. I could have dismissed his question but chose to confront the truth instead. 'I am not a fan of the brig. Nor any jail for that matter. I've spent too much time on the wrong side of the bars, and I wasn't always sure I would be getting out again.'

Lieutenant Bhukari knew what I was talking about; she'd been inside with me. So too Lieutenant Baker for that matter when the three of us along with several others were locked up while attempting to prevent a terrorist group from killing half the people on the ship with a biological weapon.

'I can't say it's my favourite place on the ship,' Deepa commented.

The elevator pinged just before the doors swished open to reveal a passageway I recognised. My stomach tightened again. 'Don't worry, Mrs Fisher,' said Baker, stepping confidently from the elevator car. 'No one will be locking you up again if we have anything to do with it.'

His confident words genuinely made me feel better, a little tension easing from my body as I followed him to the cells. There were interview rooms down here as well. It's not a nice place, but then it is not intended to be.

That a luxury cruise liner needs a brig at all is an unfortunate reflection of human nature. Even on holiday and surrounded by happiness, passengers would get into fights and need to be incarcerated until they could be charged. Violent crime was not a regular occurrence, but people were caught stealing, pickpockets came on board, and there were other crimes. A cruise ship is like a village or small town and thus has all the same problems. No one coming aboard is poor, but the range between those who could save and afford a lower level cabin, and those staying in the suites, was in the order of millions or billions and that attracted a degree of crime.

The crew were also subject to the same set of maritime laws and equally able to break them. I thought about all these things to distract myself as we came into the brig itself. The walls were bright white, the bulkheads painted starkly with no trace or suggestion of décor. Directly ahead sat a large counter with a raised front edge and beyond that, offset to the left was a door made from thick steel bars.

I knew from experience that it led to a passageway where I would find the cells.

Looking inside through the primary entrance to the brig, the door was electronically locked from the inside and had to be released by a woman at a desk. Dressed the same as Baker and Bhukari, she was either new, or one of the crew I was yet to meet.

'Patricia Fisher,' I offered her my hand once we were inside.

'Lieutenant Rudman,' she replied, gripping my hand firmly but not crushing it. 'I know who you are, of course, Mrs Fisher.'

Her accent caught me off guard. Lieutenant Rudman was in her later twenties with jet black hair pulled back tightly into a bun at the back of her head. Of Caribbean descent, Haitian perhaps if my ability to identify racial heritage from bone structure had any merit, what I noted most was that I recognised the geography of her words. They were the same as mine.

'You're from Kent?' I asked, showing my surprise.

She grinned and a small chuckle escaped her lips. 'I'm from Maidstone. That's just a couple of miles from you. My mum got all excited when I told her I was being transferred to the Aurelia, she's a big fan of yours.'

'I have fans?' My question made both Baker and Bhukari laugh at me.

Fortunately, there wasn't time to dwell on how I felt because Lieutenant Baker was getting on with the reason for our visit. 'Schneider is here somewhere?'

'Here,' Schneider announced himself, entering the brig's central area from a door to our left. 'Mrs Skies is in interview room two being watched by Pippin and Wierzbowski. You'll want to see this first.' In his hand he had a small book, A6 size I judged as he held it aloft. It was inside a clear plastic evidence bag.

When he laid in on the reception desk, I saw that it was not a book at all, but an electronic tablet made up to look like a book.

'It's a PDA?' I questioned. I'd never used or even owned a palm top computer and hadn't seen one in years. The emerging nineties technology quickly gave rise to iPads and other tablets that were far more versatile.

Schneider nodded.

'We had a tip to check it,' Deepa revealed.

'A tip?' I echoed.

Lieutenant Baker said, 'Sort of. Mrs Skies, that's Niamh Skies, August's wife, made a comment about making sure we check Evelyn's PDA because she writes everything on it and manages everyone's schedules.' I remembered her earlier comment about organising everyone and everything. She said something like that when she was screaming insults at Niamh.

'So you were to check it because that would prove … what?' I asked, curious to hear what the compelling part of all this might be.

Schneider replied. 'I believe Mrs Niamh Skies was attempting to show she and August were otherwise engaged when the suicide occurred.'

My brow creased. 'But I thought August was wandering around the ship alone? Surely that would have been a spur of the moment decision anyway and Evelyn had already retreated from the Prestwick Suite and couldn't have known about it.'

'All fair points,' Schneider agreed. 'When Niamh said it, it was just a throwaway comment, but when we asked Evelyn for it, she was very protective and didn't want to hand it over. So much so that I became suspicious and then we had to fight to take it from her. I thought her boyfriend was going to be a problem, but he backed down when Pippin told him to.'

'So what's on it?' Lieutenant Bhukari asked. 'A video of her doing the deed?' Schneider claimed the evidence was compelling but that would be more than any of us could expect or hope for.

The tall Austrian was already wearing latex gloves to handle the device which thankfully wasn't touch sensitive like modern devices. It came with a stylus that tucked into a crevice on the side. Using it, he opened the screen and then went to a folder in which he produced a file. The device was the type on which a person wrote in free hand which it then converted to text. I had to imagine that took some training for both parties to avoid the words appearing as gibberish but when Schneider stepped back so we could see the screen, it was exactly as he claimed: compelling.

My eyes danced back and forward across the screen, reading the words. Beside me, Lieutenant Baker got to the end and snorted out a choked noise of shock. On the other side of him, pressed in close so she could also read the small screen, his intended, Deepa Bhukari uttered an unladylike word.

I had to agree with her.

Meeting Lieutenant Schneider's eyes, I said, 'I assumed you challenged her on this.'

'She denies ever seeing it before,' His reply did not surprise me. 'She says she didn't write it and had nothing against the victim.'

Baker cast his eyes back down at the screen again, the damning evidence patiently waiting to be read by anyone who might wish to view it. With a shake of his head, he said, 'I don't think we will need anything more than this. We'll interview her anyway, but this is an open and shut case.'

'You're going through now?' asked Lieutenant Rudman, poised to operate the door locks.

Interview with an Innocent Woman

Mrs Skies, otherwise known as Evelyn the Ex, sat behind the desk in interview room two. Her arms were crossed to compliment her angry frown. Pippin stood to the left of the door, Lieutenant Wierzbowski, who I didn't know, to the right. No one was speaking.

Though I am not employed in any official capacity yet, Baker and the others had asked me to lead the questioning, so that was what I was going to do.

'I want a lawyer!' snapped Evelyn the Ex the moment we came into the room.

Like the rest of the brig, the walls were painted stark white and were made of steel. No thought or expense went into making the place look nice. The interior space was ten feet by ten feet and maybe eight feet high. Apart from the desk and three chairs, there was nothing in the room.

Choosing to frustrate the suspect by acting as if I hadn't even heard the comment, I came into the room, took my time shucking my jacket and setting down my handbag and then slid into one of the two chairs facing Evelyn.

She had a sea of faces looking her way now, which I knew having been on the receiving end, would be making her feel quite uncomfortable.

'I want a lawyer,' she repeated, this time with a little less venom so it sounded more like a plea than a demand.

I locked eyes with her. 'I'm afraid that is not going to happen. You are at sea and subject to a completely different set of laws. Your rights here are not the same as they are on land.' I could have told her that she could simply refuse to speak until we made land again and handed her over, but I wasn't breaking any rules by leaving that part out and she would have been read her rights by Schneider when he took her into custody. 'I want to talk to you about this document on your PDA.'

Lieutenant Schneider dutifully stepped in with the PDA which was back in the evidence bag but showing the file he found.

Evelyn glared at me. 'I already told your men; I've never seen that before and I certainly didn't write it.'

I drew in a slow breath and read it aloud. '"How to get away with murder." That's an interesting title. "Encourage Vanessa to mix alcohol and her supply of oxy. Champagne may be best as it will speed the effects of the alcohol. Once suitably pliant, encourage her to take a bath, then use a rag soaked in paint thinners to cause unconsciousness. Important to not leave bruising – she must not fight while the paint thinners subdue her. The scent of paint thinner will be present if August is painting and will not be questioned. Using Vanessa's own razor, slice both wrists and leave her to bleed out in the bath."'

I looked up from the screen to find Evelyn's eyes again. 'Well done, you can read,' she sneered. 'I still didn't write it and I had no reason to kill Vanessa.'

'What is your relationship like with the current Mrs Skies?' I already knew the answer to that one having seen their dynamic twice today, but I was curious to hear what she might say.

Caught a little off guard by my change in direction, she frowned. 'I loathe her. She stole my husband and continues to flaunt her victory in my face. If you want to look for someone who might wish to kill Vanessa, it's her you ought to be talking to.'

'Why is that?' I asked.

A smile curved the corners of Evelyn's mouth. 'Because Vanessa was doing the exact same thing to Niamh that she did to me twenty years ago: stealing her husband. August is besotted with Vanessa. Or he was,' she added as an afterthought.

'Surely, if that is the case, Niamh will just divorce August and move on with her life. Murder seems like an extreme step to take.' I thought of my own philandering husband, silently acknowledging a desire to throttle him. Thinking it and doing it are two very different things though.

However, Evelyn laughed at the suggestion of divorce. 'Ha! What do you think that would get her? The man has no money and refuses to sell his art. When I left, I thought I would be able to force a share of his material assets. I was right, but while the court awarded me half of his paintings at the time of our divorce, I am not allowed to sell any of them without his permission. They possess only conceptual worth. He survives on contributions from devoted fans and manages to live a life of luxury because he exchanges his commissions for non-monetary gifts.'

'Such as?' I prompted.

'Such as three houses. One in Paris, one in London, and one in St Lucia, but he doesn't own any of them. With each one, he insisted the deeds remain in the name of the owner, but he got stewardship to come and go at his leisure. They are his but he doesn't own them.'

Picking up on her tone, I said, 'This appears to be a source of frustration for you, Mrs Skies.'

She sagged in her chair. 'I left him. I divorced him. But I'm still shackled to him. I left with nothing of worth except the paintings and he makes me jump through hoops to gain his permission to sell one periodically. Worse yet, he gets to dictate which I can sell, and it is never from his more popular works. He is the most frustrating person on the planet. If I wanted to kill someone, it would be him.'

That was quite the statement. I logged it away for future use and swung back to the murder at hand. 'Who else could have entered that note on your PDA?'

A grimace crossed her face, something resembling anger at her situation. 'I don't know. The device is always in my possession. Clearly someone got to it, but I don't who or how or when.'

The interview went on for another hour, my questions probing as I built up a picture of the day's events and the relationship dynamics in the group.

Evelyn continued to deny any part in Vanessa's death, and I found myself willing to believe her. There were two major challenges in charging her with anything: I could find no motive for wanting the girl dead, and I was yet to prove Vanessa's death was even murder. I needed to read the autopsy report but on the face of it, the only reason any of us believed it might not be suicide was the note on Evelyn's PDA. It was utterly damning.

If Evelyn wanted to get away with murder, the last thing she wanted to do was write down how she planned to do it and then execute it in exactly that manner. I could imagine Niamh, August's current wife, wanting Vanessa dead, especially if she truly believed he was going to ditch her for the younger woman, but there was no evidence yet to suggest that was going to happen and Niamh had an ironclad alibi.

There was more work to do, but there was nothing more I could get from Evelyn the Ex. Once the interview was terminated, I waited outside with Rudman for Lieutenant Baker to finish up. Until I could prove otherwise, Evelyn was going to have to stay in the brig, the single piece of evidence against her was too much for me to overcome. That I believed she was innocent told me one thing: the note on her PDA was out there for us to find, and that had to mean Vanessa was murdered.

The security guards working in the brig would process her, stripping her of anything she could use to harm herself and would look after her as a prisoner until we reached Southampton. She would be treated fairly, but it was still an awful thing to happen if she was innocent.

Staring at nothing other than the inside of my head, the sound of the brig's entrance door opening almost startled me. I turned to find Alistair coming through the door.

'Patricia are you finished?' he enquired, surprised to find me not with the prisoner.

I gave him a lopsided smile. 'Not even nearly. It might have been suicide, but my gut tells me otherwise.' I told him about the note on Evelyn's PDA. 'I don't think she did it though. I think it's a frame.'

'How will you prove that?' he asked.

His question drew a tired snort of laughter from me. 'I have no idea.'

The door leading to the interview rooms opened, Lieutenants Baker, Bhukari, Schneider, and Pippin all coming through it. They were chattering between themselves, discussing the latest case until they spotted their captain. Alistair received several crisp salutes.

He was not in uniform but acknowledged his crew with a dip of his head. 'Well done, everyone. I hear you have something of a mystery to solve now.'

'Yes, sir,' replied Lieutenant Bhukari. 'And we don't have much time to get it done.'

Autopsy Report

Walking back to catch an elevator, I thought about what needed to happen next. Arguably, the first priority had to be determining if Vanessa's death was even a murder and for that we needed to go to the sickbay. That didn't need all of us though so Bhukari and Pippin were heading back to the Prestwick Suite to check on the guys there still gathering physical evidence and to speak with August, Niamh, and Scarlet.

They would need to take them to one of the guard stations to fingerprint them and I doubted that would go down very well. Especially with August who outwardly displayed no interest nor tolerance for anything that distracted him from what he wanted to be doing. It might prove to be an unnecessary step but was also a necessary precaution. Ultimately, the case would be handed off once we reached the next port as all such cases were. The guilty persons would be tried in their home nation in this case since they were all from the same country, but we still needed to do a tidy job of gathering the evidence.

Baker and Schneider were on their way to Evelyn's cabin on the twelfth deck. That she was staying in mediocre accommodation compared with the others might have fuelled some of the arguments I heard earlier but did nothing to provide a motive for murdering Vanessa.

Alistair came with me to the sickbay, my arm looped through his as we walked along the passageway. His presence made me feel calm and relaxed which was a nice change to the tense nervousness I couldn't shift in the brig.

At the door to the sickbay, Alistair and I were met by the duty nurse. 'Nurse Inguri, good evening,' Alistair greeted the tall African woman. Her hair was clipped to short bristles which suited her and drew attention to her soft, dark features. That Alistair knew her name came as no surprise;

he seemed to know everyone on board and never forgot any of them. I'd even heard him greet passengers who had sailed with him years before and he still remembered their names as if each conversation were indelibly ingrained in his head.

The thought sent a spike of panic through me as I wondered what arguing with him might be like. Every couple will bicker about something, but how would that go for me if he could remember exactly what I said and when I said it? With a chuckle, I dismissed the concern because I could act as every wife in the history of the world: deny all knowledge and threaten grumpy silence or withdrawal of affection if he persisted to claim he was right.

'Everything all right, Patricia?'

Alistair's voice woke me from my daydream and made me realise that I'd been chuckling to myself in the sickbay just yards from a man holding the hand of his ailing elderly wife. Somewhere behind them in one of the back rooms, Dr Davis had Vanessa's body laid out and my mirth was inappropriate.

Wiping the smile instantly from my face, I set my lips to neutral and focussed on the nurse. 'I need to speak with Dr Davis about the autopsy.' I didn't need to specify which autopsy we were discussing – at least I sure hoped I didn't.

'They're in the back,' Nurse Inguri replied, swivelling smartly around in her plastic shoes to lead us through sickbay to the small theatre area behind it. The ship needed to be equipped to deal with most medical emergencies so the sickbay was fitted with a host of equipment and two surgical theatres where minor procedures could be performed. They wouldn't attempt open-heart surgery, but tending to deep lacerations, setting broken bones, dealing with heart attacks and strokes – all these maladies and more would occur, and the ship was often too far from land for there to be anyone else who could deal with it.

I really didn't want to see Vanessa's body again. Most definitely not if the autopsy were now complete and she was either cut open, or visibly stitched back together. I also didn't feel that I could voice my reluctance to go into the room currently employed for the task. Stuck between the two positions and unable to find a middle ground, I edged into the room behind Alistair with my eyes cast down.

A furtive glance soothed my beating heart because Vanessa was covered by a sheet and the weapons of the autopsy were now out of sight.

'Ah, Mrs Fisher,' said Dr Davis. 'Captain.' Alistair got a nod of the doctor's head. I don't know how long Dr Davis has been serving on the Aurelia, but he recently rose to be the senior physician when Dr Kim was murdered. I'm sure that is not the way he wanted to get the job. His hair was going grey at the sides and probably through his facial hair as well if he wasn't always clean shaven. Like Alistair, I placed him close to my age, just on the wrong side of fifty.

Just to the right of Dr Davis and sitting at a computer workstation where he was taking notes, Barbie's boyfriend Hideki turned to face us. 'Good evening,' he greeted us both.

It was the first time I had ever seen him working as a doctor. He wore a white coat, but there was no stethoscope around his neck or thermometer sticking from a breast pocket. When he turned, I noted that on his coat there were small splashes of what might be blood but could have been another bodily fluid. I chose to not think about it.

'What can you tell us?' I asked.

'It still looks like suicide,' he insisted instantly. He strode across the room, and I questioned where he was going until he reached a stainless-steel counter on the other side where a mug of coffee steamed. 'She died from massive blood loss, that much I can tell you. There was, however, water in her lungs, but only a very small amount as if she sank beneath the surface with her very last breath. The cuts to her wrists penetrated to a depth of approximately half an inch on each side. This is abnormal since almost everyone has a dominant hand. The presence of calluses on her right hand suggest she was right-handed so one might expect the cut on her left wrist to be deeper, but it would depend on which cut was performed first.'

'How so?' I enquired keen to learn.

Dr Davis sipped his coffee and cradled the cup with both hands as he talked. 'The incisions were deep enough to sever the ligaments leading to the fingers. This would have severely compromised hand control and grip, making it difficult to hold the knife to cut the second wrist no matter which she tackled first.'

'That makes it sound like murder,' I stated.

He gave a small sideways incline of his head, conceding my point but neither agreeing nor disagreeing. 'I said it would make it difficult. It would not be impossible.'

I moved on, 'What can you tell me about her stomach contents and any drugs in her system?'

'Her blood alcohol level was sufficient for me to believe she'd drunk the entire bottle of champagne.' Behind Dr Davis, Hideki silently nodded his agreement. He was the junior doctor, here to learn from a more senior physician but would endure far less demanding hours on the Aurelia when compared to working in a hospital. 'As for drugs, I can confirm she had taken oxycodone and quite a bit of it. I need additional testing to be able to determine how many tablets she might have ingested but let's say it was most likely enough to put her into a compliant state. If we believe this is suicide, then she would have needed to act quickly to take her own life before the drugs rendered her incapable. If, however, we assume she was murdered, the killer would have been able to perform the deed without her fighting back.'

'It sounds more and more like murder all the time,' I observed.

Again, Dr Davis made the small inclination with his head; neither agreeing nor disagreeing with me.

'What about paint thinner?' I asked. Dr Davis hitched a questioning eyebrow. 'We have a note on Evelyn Skies' PDA which explains exactly how she will kill Vanessa and it correlates to how she was found. It also says she would use paint thinner to induce unconsciousness. Is there any trace of it?'

Dr Davis said, 'Yes. But there is also paint on her and even I saw the rags she used to remove paint from her skin in the bin in her bathroom. I don't know how the paint got on her, but it was only a small amount.' To prove a point and because I thought I was going to get away without seeing the post-autopsy version, he yanked back the sheet to show us all her body. 'If you look closely here, you can see a small trace of paint still in her hair.'

I glanced very quickly at the dead woman's head, trying hard to not see anything else.

Dr Davis continued, 'The paint thinner I found on her face was there because she used it to clean off the paint.'

There was silence for a beat, no one coming up with anything to say. Inside my head, one question was being shouted at a loud volume – why would you bother to clean off a blob of paint if you were about to kill yourself?

An Important Phone Call

I was already feeling a little weary, largely because I hadn't got a lot of sleep over the last few days. We had been in fear of our lives trying to take down the Godmother and then celebrating last night because we had. On top of that, I was dressed for dinner which meant heels and a jacket over a little cocktail number, so hanging around not doing much in the bowels of the ship, I was getting cold and my feet were hurting.

'I need to go back to my suite before we do anything else,' I announced to Alistair as we left sickbay.

With regret in his tone, Alistair said, 'I feel I ought to check on my replacement. Just to show that I have not abandoned her to fend for herself.'

'But you also don't want her to think you are watching her every move and judging her because it might dent her confidence,' I finished the unspoken portion of his sentence.

He nodded. 'That's about right. It's a difficult balance. I remember getting my first shot at a command. It was the same thing, a two-week stint in my case, but the man I replaced then refused to leave the ship for the first five days, checking on me every few hours. Even when he finally left, he then called every few hours to see if the ship had exploded. At the end, he gave me a glowing review, but I remember feeling just how unnecessary his constant nit-picking was.'

'How do you feel now?'

He chuckled at himself. 'Like I want to watch her like a hawk. The Aurelia ... it's my responsibility. Everything about it, everyone on it, everything that happens to it. From Purple Star's point of view, once I handed over command earlier today, anything that happens is nothing to do with me, yet I am finding it a little hard to let go of the reins.'

I cupped his chin and pulled his face down for a kiss. 'I'll see if I can help to take your mind off that later.'

Back at my suite, I stifled a yawn while Jermaine took my jacket and all three dachshunds fussed around my legs. I made a point of petting each in turn, then led them to my bedroom where they each got a gravy bone as a treat.

Alistair had kissed me outside the door and left me to proceed with the investigation. He had other matters to attend to, not least of which was packing to go ashore tomorrow. The Aurelia was due to dock in Southampton at breakfast. It would sail again the following morning but not with us on board.

How long we chose to stay in England was up to us, but the ship was to visit the Mediterranean after leaving England and from there it would travel down the west coast of Africa before crossing the Atlantic for South America. We knew its route and could catch up with it whenever we wanted.

Realistically, that would be whenever my business in England was concluded and that meant settling things with my husband, Charlie. Charlie wanted half of everything I had, and his lawyers were clear that they thought he had fair claim to it. Basically, my soon to be ex-husband was a greedy pig with eyes as big as saucers and an empty pot that could never be filled no matter how much gold was poured into it.

Only once I left him did I discover how much money he'd weaselled away over the years. For years he let his wife drive around in a tatty, old second-hand Ford Fiesta with all the power of a hairdryer and as much kerb appeal as yesterday's discarded sandwiches. All the while he was squirrelling money away and making investments.

Now, having denied me my fair share for over three decades, he wanted half of everything I had. Well, I was going to make sure he got not one penny. Apart from one phone call a couple of weeks ago, I hadn't put much effort into sorting out my side of the divorce. Charlie and his lawyers knew that and were gleefully rubbing their hands together no doubt.

Now that I was free of the shadow the Godmother had cast, I could focus my efforts on where my life was going instead of worrying if I would have a life at all.

Jermaine prepared me a gin and tonic – it was now an appropriate time of the day for it – and brought it to my bedroom. At his polite knock, I said, 'Come in, please, Jermaine.'

'Your beverage, madam,' he announced, carrying a silver tray expertly with one hand.

I had my phone in my right hand and in my left, I held a business card. I passed the business card into my right so I could take the offered drink. I sipped at it, savouring the heady botanical mix. 'Thank you, Jermaine.'

He dipped his head in acknowledgement and made to leave my bedroom again.

'Jermaine.'

He turned to face me again. 'Yes, madam?'

I skewed my lips to one side, trying to work out what I wanted to ask him. 'We … I wanted to ask you about my divorce.'

His eyebrows showed surprise very briefly, but then he folded the silver tray behind his back so he was holding it with both arms and gave me his full attention.

I needed to pose an actual question now. 'You're aware that Charlie is attempting to get half the Maharaja's house in East Malling along with half of all the items inside it including the collection of cars?'

'Yes, madam. It is your house now though, is it not?'

I sighed. 'Technically, yes. Okay, so here is the question: is it bad if I let him walk himself into a pit and utterly destroy him?'

Jermaine's eyebrows rose again, showing surprise either at the question or that I was asking his opinion. 'I assume you mean financially, madam. You are able to do that?'

I nodded slowly. 'I need to make a phone call, but yes, maybe. Would that make me a bad person?'

A small snort of laughter escaped Jermaine's nose before he swiftly regained his butler's dour posture. 'It is my interpretation, madam, that your husband has no claim to that which was once the Maharaja's and has only recently become yours. That being the case, he is not entitled to any of it and,' he placed one hand on his chest to show sincerity, 'I personally feel that you should give him hell, madam.'

I had seen my butler kick people in the head – because they deserved it and were trying to kill me, of course. I had seen him dress as a woman more than once, and also pretend to be Steed from the Avengers. However, I could not remember a time when I had ever heard him use a word which some might consider to be borderline profanity.

It made a burst of laughter spring from my mouth. It was a good thing I was holding my gin and not taking a sip because I would have sprayed him with it had that been the case. As my laughter subsided, I dropped my phone and the business card, then placed the glass of gin on my dressing table so I could step forward a pace and wrap the man up in an affectionate hug.

'I do not know what I would do without you, Jermaine,' I whispered, a tear coming to my eye because when we returned to the Aurelia in a week or two weeks or whatever it was, I would be moving into the captain's quarters with Alistair and my wonderful friend and protector would be staying on as the butler in the Windsor Suite.

I held him for several seconds longer than was appropriate and didn't care because I was in my happy place and I knew he felt the same way about me.

When I broke the hug, I needed to dab at my eyes, a handkerchief appearing in Jermaine's hand as if conjured there using magic.

'Shall I prepare a second glass, madam?' he asked, backing toward my bedroom door.

I considered it but not for long. 'No thank you, sweetie. I have work to do tonight.'

After a swift glug of my gin and tonic, I called the number on the business card. It was well after office hours, but I knew from experience the person I was calling worked whatever hours he felt necessary. I'd discovered that when he was pursuing me.

When he answered, the memory of the terror I felt at our first encounter resurfaced. I swallowed it down, steadied my voice to announce myself and waited to see what he had to say.

'Ah, yes, Mrs Fisher,' his rumbling bass filled my ears. 'I was able to look into the matter and believe that you are most likely in luck.'

My heart hammered in my chest with much the same force as it might if someone aimed a gun at me. My tongue darted out to wet lips that felt all too dry suddenly. 'I will need to know within the week. I have rather a lot riding on confirmation one way or the other.'

'Yes, Mrs Fisher, I understand.' His voice held so little inflection it was hard to tell if he was excited or bored, disinterested or half dead. None of that mattered though. Confident that he knew his job and the urgency which my request carried, I bade him a goodnight and let him go. Then, with my heart still racing, I stared at my reflection in the mirror. 'You want half do you, Charlie. Let's see how that tastes, shall we?'

It Looked Different in the Pictures

The last half of my gin and tonic went in a single hit. I was dressed, I'd managed to eat enough of my evening meal before I was disturbed to not feel hungry now, and I knew I wouldn't be able to sleep yet because the mystery of Vanessa's death was going to keep me awake if I tried to go to bed.

Besides, it was barely ten o'clock, which on a luxury cruise ship meant the evening was just getting started.

Leaving my bedroom, with the dogs tucked up sleepy and happy on my bed, I found two figures waiting for me in my living room. In the lamp-lit space they caught me off guard and I squealed as my heart jumped.

'Whoa, Patty. It's just us,' sniggered Barbie. She was wearing an all in one black catsuit made from a shiny leather-like material. It hugged her figure in all the right places and had a zip at the front which started at her navel and stopped an inch beneath the underside of her boobs. It exposed a lot of flesh.

Staring at her cleavage, I tried to avoid pulling a face, but she tracked my eyes. 'Oh, yes,' she rolled her eyes. 'Jermaine bought it for me.'

'Really?' I aimed my eyes at Jermaine. He was wearing his Steed outfit again; the one he reserved for nights when he thought things might get adventurous. Jermaine liked to dress as Steed. I might have mentioned that earlier but using all the descriptive words in the world would still fail to capture the image of a six-foot four-inch Jamaican man in a fitted suit with brogues, an umbrella, and a bowler hat.

'Yes, madam,' he replied. 'Barbie and I were watching old episodes a short while ago and she admired the outfits Emma Peel wore. I thought I would treat her to one.'

Barbie pulled a face which I took to mean she was wearing it only because her best friend didn't know any better. She looked down at her chest. 'Do you think anyone will notice?'

'Notice?' I choked. 'You look like you have twin babies in there fighting to get out.'

She put her chin on her chest, staring directly down at the twin orbs of flesh heaving every time she breathed. Then she shrugged. 'Oh, well. It won't be the first time everyone looks at my boobs instead of my face.'

Jermaine's face took on a concerned look. 'Is there something wrong with the outfit?'

'When you bought it, did it say Emma Peel outside on it?' I wanted to know.

Jermaine looked worried now. 'No. I tried that but couldn't find anyone who makes them.'

'So what is this?' Barbie asked.

Even with his dark skin, I could see Jermaine's cheeks flush when he admitted. 'Slutty spy.' I snorted a burst of laughter. 'In my defence, it didn't look like this on the woman modelling it in the pictures.'

'Did she have enormous boobs?' I asked.

'Well, no,' Jermaine reluctantly admitted.

It was a dangerous outfit, but it did make her look like a large chested version of Emma Peel against Jermaine's Jamaican John Steed. I wanted to ask if they were going to a fancy dress party, but what would have been the point in that?

Instead, I asked, 'Where are you going anyway?'

'We hoped you might allow us to accompany you, madam,' said Jermaine, hooking his umbrella onto the crook of his right elbow.

Barbie shot me a smile. 'The Godmother has gone and hopefully with it the constant threat of mortal danger. With so many things changing, we wanted something to stay the same. The three of us came together to solve the first case with the sapphire. You'll be the ship's detective soon and Jermaine will have a new principle to protect.' I felt a lump form in my throat. 'This might be our last chance to solve a mystery on board together.'

An unwelcome tear rolled down my right cheek.

The magic handkerchief appeared again.

'How am I supposed to say no to that?' I blubbed, my voice betraying my command to come out strong and confident. I didn't want the team to break up.

Gasping to get my breathing under control and drive away all the negative emotions, I felt like I'd been watching a marathon of sad movies. 'We need to collect Sam,' I insisted. I couldn't spend the next few hours digging into Vanessa's death in a state of sodden misery and it was almost impossible to not be in a good mood around Sam.

'We already called him,' Barbie revealed. 'Where are we going first? Jermaine will collect him.'

The answer came at the flip of a mental coin. It had been two hours since I left the brig and sent the teams away to check on Evelyn's cabin and the Prestwick Suite. I'd heard nothing from either pair since, but enough time had passed for both to be able to have something to report, even if it was that there was nothing to find.

Picking the farthest spot first, I said, 'Let's go to deck twelve.

Secret Phone

My two good friends started working on the case long before they surprised me with their request to join in. While I was in the brig interviewing Evelyn the Ex and then in sickbay speaking with Dr Davis, Barbie and Jermaine were bringing themselves up to speed with the persons involved and doing some research.

It always struck me as odd that Barbie, a woman of action, was so at home spending hours picking through pages and pages of information to find the details she needed.

On the way to Evelyn's cabin on deck twelve, she told me what she knew so far. 'The boyfriend's name is Eoin Planchet.' I already knew this, of course, but I let her continue without interrupting. She said it as Owen, and then spelled it out. 'I couldn't work out how to say it and had to look it up. Irish names are funny. Anyway, Eoin is forty-nine years old,' which made him older than I thought but not by much. 'He is a professional bodybuilder who almost made it to the big time but never quite got there. He's had some minor acting roles and still competes in the seniors' category. Now he owns a bunch of gyms in the Dublin area.

'How did he end up with Evelyn Skies?'

Barbie just shrugged. 'That one I cannot tell you.'

'Any idea how long they have been dating?' I was full of questions.

This time she shook her head. 'No idea. We can ask him that though.'

When we arrived in the right passageway, we found Baker and Schneider coming out of a cabin door a few yards ahead of us. Baker had his radio up to his face but lowered it again when he saw me.

'I was just about to call you, Mrs Fisher.' He spotted Barbie in her racy outfit and had to force his eyes away because there was no safe part of her to look at apart from maybe her feet and the top of her head. I saw him mouth, 'Wow,' in an uncomfortable way.

'Are you all done in there?' I asked.

Schneider also caught a look at Barbie and decided the painting on the wall next to him was worthy of focussed inspection.

Chuckling, Barbie said, 'You guys are so goofy.'

She was dealing with her outfit problems, but I had to imagine Jermaine was going to get a talking to later. I suspected it would be a while before he tried to surprise his friend with a gift of clothing again.

To answer my question and probably so he could look at me rather than fight against his eyes which were being drawn like magnets toward Barbie's ample cleavage, Baker said, 'Yes. Mr Planchet can account for his whereabouts since coming on board. We quizzed him back and forth, but he stated that he has not yet been inside the Prestwick Suite. He is only here to accompany Evelyn on her trip. Since she was to be working today on organising August's life, he took himself to the gym, which we were able to corroborate already – he went to the weights studio on deck fourteen,' Barbie nodded appreciatively, 'then went for dinner in the Argentinian Steakhouse on deck eighteen. Again, we were able to confirm he was there. There are a couple of holes in the timeline where he could have gone somewhere or done something, but I don't think he is involved.'

Schneider said, 'He didn't even know Vanessa was dead or that Evelyn had left the Prestwick Suite. He wasn't here when we took her into custody; that was during the time he spent at the gym.'

Baker admitted, 'We were a little clumsy in breaking the news.' He made a half shrug. 'I figured he must have already known.'

'What's in the bag?' I asked, seeing something black and shiny in an evidence bag dangling from Schneider's right hand.

'Ah, well, this is the interesting bit,' said Baker as Schneider held the object aloft.

'It's his phone?' I sought to confirm, guessing there was something on it that would help us work out if Vanessa had been murdered or not.

Schneider shook his head knowingly while Baker said, 'No. Not exactly. According to Eoin Planchet, this is Vanessa's second phone.'

'Second phone?' Barbie echoed. 'Vanessa had a second phone?'

Lieutenant Baker nodded. 'Mr Planchet claims to be holding it for her. He didn't know why, though he suggested it was because August Skies is a very jealous man and constantly checks up on who the women are talking to. If Mr Planchet is to be believed, August Skies doesn't often let the two young women out of his sight, so when Vanessa begged Mr Planchet to hold this for her, he agreed without question.'

'And he just gave it up?' Barbie asked.

'Mrs Fisher,' called Sam Chalk, my assistant, as he and Jermaine found us. They were coming along the corridor from the direction of the nearest elevators. Now there were six of us in the passageway and clearly making too much noise because the door to Mr Planchet's cabin opened.

'I can hear every word you are saying,' he commented, his Irish lilt delighting my ears. 'Since I am the current focus of this discussion, I might as well be part of it. Please ask whatever questions you wish. I have nothing to hide.'

I pointed to the phone. 'What's on it?' I wanted to know.

His forehead creased a little. 'It's not my phone.'

Baker grimaced. 'It has a fingerprint lock. We already tried to open it.'

Eoin loomed in his doorway, far bigger now I was up close to him than he had seemed on the quayside. He wasn't that he was tall, though he was over six feet, so much as he was broad. They say about men being barrel chested, but never had it seemed more fitting. Dressed in grey flannel slouch pants and a vest, the kind that bodybuilders wear that consist of almost no material, his muscles heaved and rolled each time he moved. It was as if there wasn't enough space for them under his skin and they constantly had to get out of the way of each other.

'I kept it for Vanessa, that was all. It never once occurred to me to try to open it so I could snoop on her. She found the chance to get it from me most days. I'm not sure who she was messaging but I believe that is what she was doing. I saw her on several occasions. She would open the phone and read whatever messages she had. Then she would type a reply or two and then wait, nervously checking to see if August would appear, or that cow Scarlet. That she was terrified of getting caught with it was obvious. Sometimes she would get a message back straight away; the phone would ping, and sometimes not.'

'And you've no idea who she was messaging?' I was desperate to know.

He shook his head, the overdeveloped trapezius muscles either side of his neck shifting each time it went left and then right. 'It could have been a sick grandparent or a child she left behind, a boyfriend or a sister. She never spoke of it and I never felt I had a right to ask. She would have brought the subject up had she wanted to discuss it.'

I admired his approach to the young woman; helping her while not prying. Assuming he was telling me the truth, that is.

'How long ago did she give you the phone?' Jermaine asked. It was a question I wanted the answer to, but my mind had chosen to drift back to another thing he had said. I stuck a pin in it, hoping I would circle back and not get too distracted.

'Just a couple of weeks,' Eoin replied without hesitation. 'I had just returned from the gym, so it was a Saturday morning.'

Barbie's face was scrunched up with doubt. 'Do you all live together or something?'

Eoin chuckled. 'You want to know how Vanessa would even know me, right? I live next door to August. I have done for years. That's how I got to know Evelyn. Before Vanessa approached me with the phone, we had exchanged no more than a handful of words. We still haven't, I guess. And now we never will.' His last words were tinged with sadness for the young woman.

I needed to see what was on the phone and it was now my highest priority.

As if hearing my thoughts, Baker said, 'The only way to see what is on this phone is to use Vanessa's fingerprint to open it.'

Barbie screwed up her face. 'Ewwww.'

I pulled a face too – I didn't want that job.

Schneider saw my expression. 'Don't worry, Mrs Fisher. We will have one of the medics do it. The dead deserve all the respect we can give them.'

The conversation lulled, everyone falling silent for a moment. Eoin took a step back from his cabin door, aiming to go back inside. 'Evelyn didn't do it, you know. Scarlet might have, but Evelyn wouldn't hurt a fly.'

There it was again. He'd called her a cow a moment ago though from the brief amount of time I spent in her company, I got the impression she and Vanessa were good friends. If she had been faking her tears earlier, she did a good job of it.

I was about to ask him about Scarlet when Sam raised his hand. 'You don't have to raise your hand, sweetie,' I coached.

'Yes, Mrs Fisher,' he replied obediently as he lowered it again. 'I thought Mrs Skies had written out how she was going to murder Vanessa.'

I watched Eoin's face to see how he might react to the accusation. He cast his eyes down at the deck. 'The gentlemen asked me what I knew about that,' he said, indicating Baker and Schneider with a nod of his head. Looking back up to meet my eyes, he continued, 'They wanted to know if Evelyn ever talked about Vanessa in negative terms or expressed any desire to hurt her. I told them the same thing I am going to tell you. Evelyn wouldn't hurt a fly. If Vanessa's death wasn't suicide, then you have the wrong person in custody.'

I believed that he believed what he was saying. That I also believed he was right, I kept to myself. 'How about Scarlet?' I asked. 'What does Evelyn think of her?'

A look of distaste crossed Eoin's face at the mention of Scarlet's name. 'Evelyn didn't like to make negative comments,' he replied, giving nothing away.

'But you have,' I pointed out. 'You called her a cow a few minutes ago. Why is that?'

Seeing that he was trapped by his own words, Eoin confessed, 'She came across as manipulative. I don't think she ever had a genuine emotion. I believe she saw Vanessa as a rival both for August's attention and his affection and she pretended to be Vanessa's friend while carefully making sure August watched Vanessa more closely and restricted her movements more stringently. When Vanessa first brought me her phone, I thought she was hiding it from August. Now I'm not so sure she wasn't hiding it from Scarlet just as much if not more.'

'We need to speak with Scarlet, then, don't we, Mrs Fisher,' said Sam, voicing an obvious conclusion.

I drew in a slow deep breath through my nose, inflating my lungs as I considered what needed to happen next. A yawn threatened to split my face, subsiding when I kept my teeth clamped together. As the need to yawn dissipated, I said, 'Thank you, Mr Planchet. If you think of anything else you feel may be pertinent to our investigation, however insignificant it may seem, please contact us. You can do that via any member of the crew.'

He bade us goodnight, closed his door, and left the six of us in the passageway.

I really wanted to grill Scarlet and August about Vanessa, but there was something more pressing now. 'We need to check out what is on that phone.'

There is Such a Thing as Too Distracting

Lieutenant Baker let the security guards in the Prestwick Suite know we were making a detour and got caught up on how their work was going. The chaps doing the forensic work – the ship's security team have to be self-sufficient – were almost finished and hadn't yet found anything they considered worthy of note.

When I asked him to, Baker passed on my request for Bhukari and whoever else was there to hold off on the interviews until we knew more. He told them about the secret phone, the suggestion that it might contain incriminating evidence didn't need to be voiced.

I had no desire to go back to sickbay and the sad body lying under the sheet, but that was what we needed to do. Sure, I could send Baker and Schneider, but I didn't want to get into a habit of passing on tasks that I could do myself just because they were unsavoury.

We were heading for an elevator to get to sickbay again when we were spotted.

'I said we would find them if we looked.' The voice came from behind me as into the passageway shuffled first Rick, who had spoken, then Akamu. On their shoulder was Mike Atwell. The three men had a rosy glow to their cheeks that suggested several beverages had been imbibed this evening.

'We missed you, Patty,' moaned Akamu good naturedly. 'This was supposed to be our farewell.'

'Don't say anything,' interrupted Mike, his instruction aimed at me I thought, but probably extended to Barbie, Baker, and Schneider as they were standing next to me. 'We've got a small wager going.'

I hitched an eyebrow, not sure I liked where this might be going. 'What are you rogues up to?'

Next to me, Barbie turned around to face the oncoming trio of mature men and all their chattering stopped. The alcohol had diminished their social consciousness and eroded their sense of propriety, so now all three were staring at my blonde friend's voluminous chest.

No one said anything for a second until Barbie tutted. 'Guys, my eyes are up here.'

Rick didn't bother to look up when he replied. 'Yes, Barbie, I'm sure they are but ... it looks like two bald men pressing their foreheads together,' he muttered in wonder.

Barbie tutted again and tugged ineffectually at the zip to see if it would go up a little further. When it didn't, she turned through ninety degrees and yanked at the material, pulling it upwards to see if her flesh would settle a little lower.

Unfortunately, having turned away from Rick, Mike, and Akamu, she was jiggling her boobs right in the faces of Baker and Schneider.

I took my jacket off with a sigh. 'Here, try this.'

Really, she needed to put it on backwards so she could completely cover herself, because even with the jacket around her, most of her boobs were still on display.

Trying to move the conversation on, I prompted, 'You were saying something about a wager?'

'Well, after the ladies departed, we got to talking about old cases,' explained Mike.

'Young'un here,' Rick hitched a finger at Mike. I was willing to bet Mike hadn't been called young in a while. 'He wanted to bet that you rushed off to investigate a murder.'

Akamu interrupted his Hawaiian partner, 'Whereas I believe it was more likely to be a double murder.'

'Then we got to discussing the intricacies of the crime,' said Rick. 'How the murder was perpetrated, whether the driver was sex or money or revenge.'

Feeling a need to cut this short before the three dozy drunks rambled on for too long, I asked, 'And what was the end result of all this discussion?'

'I said it would be a rich widow being murdered by a gigolo for her jewellery,' stated Akamu boldly.

'Not even close,' I shot him down and got to watch his smile fall while Rick elbowed him in the ribs.

Mike went next. 'I guessed it would be teenage lovers found intwined after taking part in a suicide pact because their parents refused to let them be together.'

I pursed my lips, considering how to score his attempt. 'Close, but no banana, Mike.' He looked genuinely disappointed.

Rick, clown that he likes to be, especially when he's had a few, could barely stop himself from laughing while he tried to tell me his guess. 'I said you'd already had all the mundane cases, and this was bound to be something more spectacular,' he giggled.

'Go on,' my eyes were narrowed, wondering what he might say.

'Well Mike was telling us about that Tempest Michaels chap and the cases you solved with him. So I figured it was probably a nest of undead ninja assassins travelling to Stonehenge in England to bring about the apocalypse and they were making human sacrifices as part of their build up to the ritual.' He was laughing so hard by the end that he had to put an arm against the bulkhead to keep himself upright.

I shook my head at him. 'That's actually really close, Rick,' I told him with a sad and fearful edge to my voice. 'Someone is making ritual sacrifices. We've discovered six so far.'

Rick's laughter shut off in an instant and the two men with him gawped with open mouths to hear what I would say next.

'You're kidding,' said Rick, the timbre of his voice pleading for it to not be true.

I held up my phone and took a picture. 'Got you.'

Rick sagged against the bulkhead, a hand on his heart. 'Goodness, you can't do that to an old man.'

'Serves you right,' I told him. 'Now get to bed, you reprobates.'

I air-kissed all three goodnight, as did Barbie while trying to keep her chest out of the equation, and we watched briefly as they shuffled off along the passageway again, chuckling to each other.

A Secret Well Kept

'You want to do what?' asked Nurse Inguri, her eyes wide at Lieutenant Baker's request.

'It's the only way to unlock the phone,' I told her.

That she didn't like the idea of messing with the corpse lying on the autopsy table a few yards behind her was neither here nor there. We were going to do it. Having her assist rather than resist was going to make it easier but it wasn't necessary.

Through the door that led to the surgical rooms beyond, Hideki poked his head.

Barbie waved her hand enthusiastically, 'Hey, babe.'

Sam copied her, 'Hey, babe.'

Hideki raised an eyebrow. 'Good evening, everyone. Did you have more questions about Miss Morton? Dr Davis has retired, I'm afraid.'

Barbie went around Nurse Inguri to get to her boyfriend, putting her arms around him to plant a swift kiss on his lips. 'I'm sure you can help us, babe. We just need a fingerprint.'

The request required nothing more than Lieutenant Schneider holding up the phone in the evidence bag for Hideki to understand what was needed. He stepped back and held the door open, inviting us to go to the body with him.

I held back, content at this stage to let someone else do the icky part. As Schneider took the bag with the phone forward, I mused to myself that being married to Charlie for all those years I ought to be used to touching a dead body. It brought a flicker of a smile to my face, my thoughts drifting back to the divorce and the impending meeting with his team of lawyers.

Charlie's lawyers were going to offer me paperwork to sign; they'd told me as much already. They thought this was a simple case of splitting the assets down the middle, but it wasn't. Just as my thoughts were darkening and I could feel my face beginning to form an angry mask, Schneider re-emerged, the phone in his hand now lit.

Feet shot forward to see, not just mine but everyone in the room, Nurse Inguri included. The result, of course, was that no one could really see anything.

Schneider backed away a pace and lifted the phone in the air, then turned around so we were all facing the same way and could look up at it above his head.

'There is only one number in the phone's contact list,' he told us, flicking between the different functions. 'No name, just a number.' He went into the call log. 'No calls made from this phone ever. Just messages by the look of it.' He switched function again, opening the text messaging service.

Again, there was only one entry and it was just a number. 'The messages go back a month almost. This will take a while to go through.'

His scrolling finger whizzed through the reem of messages, showing us there were hundreds of them. He went back to the start, to the very first message sent.

'B, this is my number now. I got a new phone. August doesn't know about it. Only use this number now, babe. I'll keep it hidden and check on you every day if I can. I will escape him, and we can be together.'

The message was from her to someone referred to as B. In those few words, she told us all we might need to know about her relationship with August. That he had a hold over her was unquestioned now, though how he achieved it was yet to be discovered. She wanted to escape – that was the word she used – and she was keeping whoever B was a secret.

The next message was a response from B. *'It crushes me that we cannot yet be together. I know it will be soon, and I will be waiting for you as we previously discussed. Fear not, my love, for when you reach my shores, your flight from his clutches will be assured.'*

We read several more, barely a word being spoken for more than five minutes as Schneider opened each message in turn. For me, a picture was forming. Vanessa had met someone. Whether that was through an online chat room, an internet dating website that matched people, or whether she had physically met him, B was someone she knew. A male someone from the gist of the messages.

They were in love, if the messages could be believed, and she was on her way to him. Somehow, the trip around the world on the Aurelia was going to put her wherever he was, and she would run away from August at that point.

She didn't get the chance. I shook my head. 'This was no suicide.' No one argued with me.

'Do I call the number?' asked Lieutenant Schneider.

I pinched at my bottom lip with forefinger and thumb, lost in thought. If we identified who B was, would that help us? Was B real? I had no reason to believe otherwise but when I formed the question, I got a familiar itch at the back of my skull.

Everyone was looking my way, waiting to hear what I would say next. I nodded, 'Yes, I think we should see if it is answered, but we need to be guarded about what we say. B could be the killer for all we know.'

Sam asked the perfect question. 'Won't it tip them off if they are the killer?'

I patted his shoulder. 'That's the risk we have to take.'

Lieutenant Schneider pressed the green button, connecting the call. 'Who is going to talk if he answers?'

No one volunteered, then Baker, Barbie, and I all spoke up at the same time. Ultimately, it didn't matter because the phone rang and rang and eventually went to voicemail.

Covering the microphone port with a finger, Schneider hissed, 'Disconnect or leave a message?' I mimed cutting the call by waving a flat hand across my neck.

'No one answered, what does that mean?' asked Barbie, voicing a question I think we all wanted an answer to.

Thinking aloud, I said, 'It could mean anything. There's no point reading anything into it yet. What we must do, is go to the Prestwick Suite to speak with August Skies. We didn't get a confession from Evelyn as I hoped we might and though the verdict is still technically suicide, I no longer believe it.' I turned to Barbie, 'Babes, you're a whizz with this stuff. Can you dig through all those messages and see if B's identity is revealed anywhere? I know this is a pile of work.'

She waved me into submission. 'You're right, Patty. I am a whizz at this. I could do with a helper though. I'll need to transcribe anything that seems of interest. There might be a location listed or something to suggest how they came to meet each other.'

'I can assist, madam,' said Jermaine, volunteering to go with his best friend. They worked well together, that much was proven.

'The rest of us will head to the Prestwick Suite. There is much that I wish to ask August Skies.'

Narcissistic Pig

At the Prestwick Suite Bhukari and Pippin were trying to finish what they were doing. However, there was more to find and catalogue than in Eoin and Evelyn's cabin. The champagne bottle had been dusted for prints, so too most of the other items in the adjoining bathroom of Vanessa's bedroom. We came inside to find the team doing the forensic gathering still hard at work even though it was getting late for the occupants of the suite.

'We've arranged alternative accommodation for them,' Lieutenant Bhukari told us, her voice quiet. 'I wouldn't want to stay in here now if someone I knew had just died. Suicide or murder, it would give me the creeps either way.'

'They don't want to go?' asked Sam.

Deepa shook her head. 'Scarlet wanted to, but August said one word and she changed her mind. One word,' she repeated. 'All he had to say was "No" and she changed her mind on the spot. It was bizarre to witness, like he had some kind of control over her.'

'Mrs Skies decided to stay as well?' I asked.

'She's out cold,' Pippin remarked. 'She put away a bottle of whiskey — Irish whiskey naturally — and had to be carried to her bed.'

Bhukari narrowed her eyes at the artist whose back was to us as he worked on a different painting to the one of Scarlet I saw earlier. 'Not that her husband was of any help. All August has done is paint. It's as if he isn't aware of anything happening around him.'

I watched him now for a moment. The canvas of Scarlet's tearful face was to his right, placed against a wall to finish drying. On the easel now, a new painting, this time of the Aurelia which he was creating using a series of large photographs. In his right hand he had a small trowel, the type I would expect to see a builder using to lay cement, only smaller.

Curious, I approached him. Deepa tapped my arm to get my attention before I'd taken the first pace in his direction.

'I wouldn't bother until he is finished,' she whispered. 'All he's done when we attempted to speak to him this evening was shush us and promise that he would call the owners of Purple Star and have us fired if we disturbed him again.'

Pippin added, 'He did say he would give us the time we needed when he was finished.'

Good luck getting me fired, August Skies. With nothing to fear, I walked over to stop next to him, a little too close for him to have room to move. 'No brush this time, Mr Skies?'

I got a flicker of annoyance from him, but his little trowel paused in the air. 'The trowel gives greater depth when needed. I employ it here to give me texture and to blend colours. I can work faster,' he glanced over his shoulder at the security team, 'something your philistine colleagues deem of value. Are you an artist, Mrs Fisher?'

I gave a small shake of my head, never letting my eyes leave his canvas. The image coming to life by his hand was quite remarkable. Vivid colours spread across the flat surface to give depth. 'It is not a skill I am fortunate enough to possess.' He hadn't spoken to anyone for hours, choosing to be rude and hostile instead, but now he was talking to me. Was that just because I had enquired about his work? 'I see you are painting from still images, could you not have done this at your studio, wherever that is?'

His face registered surprise, glancing at the part finished painting and then back at me as if confused by my question. 'This is just a practice piece, Mrs Fisher. Nothing but a few mindless daubs of paint. I shall paint over it in the morning.'

'Practice piece?'

He stared at the painting, waving his trowel here and there to draw my attention as he spoke. 'The dimensions are off, the light is wrong … no, I would never let anyone see this shoddy attempt. To capture the ship in all its majesty, as is the commission I have undertaken, I must have natural light, not what the photographer saw, and as you can see, I am producing this child's attempt using multiple photographs taken in different locations – it would be impossible to get the light right.'

I understood the point he was trying to make about the light, but to my untrained eye, the ship and everything he had painted so far looked utterly perfect. In that moment, I wanted to offer him money for his practice piece so I could hang it on my wall.

Having lapsed into silence, he restarted painting, a swift right hand darting to his palette of oil paints and then back to the canvas to add a long swipe of a dark blue. With one sweep of his hand, there were waves, and in the next second, delicate white caps appeared to give the waves a sense of the sun catching on the crests.

It was stunning to watch, and I was mesmerised for a few seconds. Finally coming back to my senses, I remembered that I needed to steer him off the subject of his painting.

He was already talking again, holding his palette knife to the ceiling, and squinting at it critically. 'The secret to palette knife work is to get the right edge.' He paused, a wry smile fleetingly appearing and vanishing again. 'Mrs Fisher you have asked me more about my craft than any of my lovers have. Even my wives have never really taken any interest. They extend platitudes because they must, but they have never really bothered to learn anything.' he brought the trowel thing into the light again. 'Most artists just use them as they are sold, but a straight edge on both sides limits the ability to manipulate the paint once it is on the canvas. I have these shaped specifically for me,' he boasted, twisting the little tool so I could see the scimitar curve along one edge. 'This one isn't quite right though, which is why this feeble attempt is so unspeakably embarrassing.'

Without a further word, and with no warning, he switched his grip to hold the little knife *Psycho* style above his head, then stabbed it savagely down into the canvas.

It made me gasp and dance away, backing to my right to get some distance between myself and the crazy artist as he hacked and slashed at the painting I would happily have paid money for. Unsatisfied with just killing the painting, he then kicked out the leg of the easel so it toppled backward, spilling the canvas onto the kitchen's tiled floor. Then he threw down his palette of paints and stormed to the kitchen.

'Niamh!' His shout filled the otherwise quiet cabin. 'Niamh!' He was shouting for his wife, his tone angry and his expression impatient as if she were deliberately making him wait.

'She's gone to bed, Mr Skies,' I explained loudly, assuming the man somehow didn't know. When his mouth then stopped halfway through opening to shout her name again, I said, 'We need to interview you now, Mr Skies. Please do not make me have ship's security take you into custody.'

'Interview me? Evelyn manages all my press and marketing. You'll have to make an appointment with her.'

Was he messing with me? 'Not that kind of interview, Mr Skies. This is about Vanessa's death.'

His face froze for a second, making it look as if he were checking with his memory. 'Ah, yes. She committed suicide earlier. A terrible waste. What is it you wish to ask me?'

I nodded my head at Lieutenant Baker; it was time to get a few answers from the man at the middle of this mystery. 'Let's move into the kitchen, shall we.'

Apart from the chaps in Vanessa's bedroom still cataloguing her possessions and looking through her laptop, it was just the four members of the security team, myself, and August. Scarlet was asleep presumably, though we would have to wake her for a chat before we left, and Niamh. If Niamh had drunk herself into a stupor, interviewing her might have to wait until morning.

Retiring to the breakfast bar, young Lieutenant Pippin offered to make coffee for everyone. I watched to see where August would choose to sit, then positioned myself opposite so I could look right into his eyes.

He got no time to get comfortable before I hit him with the first question. 'Why would Vanessa kill herself?'

August's eyes flared wide. 'I cannot imagine, Mrs Fisher. To the best of my knowledge I made her happy. She had everything she needed in life.'

'How about a future?' I challenged him.

August tilted his head while frowning deeply. 'What do you mean by that?'

'A future,' I repeated. 'You are forty-six years older than her, by all accounts a womaniser, and already married. Did it never once occur to you that she might want to meet someone who could become her husband, or that she might want children? What about financial security? You may care for her needs now, but what about in a few years' time when you find a younger woman? How is she to support herself when she has no career? Did you plan to give her a large golden handshake when you were done with her?'

I was goading August and he was bright enough to see it. 'The women in my life are with me of their own choosing. They choose to come to me, for the fame it gives them. Many have gone on to successful modelling careers, one even went into acting, scoring a series of television roles. I love them, and only ask that they love me in return.'

'But what if she wanted to leave?' I pestered.

August disliked the question. 'Why would she?'

'Humour me, please. What if she announced a desire to leave you? What if she had met someone else?'

'Unthinkable,' he sputtered dismissively. 'Next question.'

I narrowed my eyes. 'No, I think I'll stick with this one. I think you knew she was planning to leave.' I couldn't tell you why, but I wanted August to be guilty of Vanessa's murder, and if he knew about B, I already had a reason why he might want to. He was glaring back at me now, unhappy at being accused. 'I think you knew she was in contact with someone else and you didn't like it. Tell me, August, when did a woman last leave you?'

His glare intensified, his nostrils flaring at the indignity of my question. 'Why would a woman ever want to leave me?' he wanted to know.

I snorted. 'You're not much to look at, August. Hardly an Adonis. A better question might be how you manage to talk such young beauties into your bed in the first place.'

August jutted his face across the table, getting it close enough to mine that I could smell the coffee on his breath. 'I don't talk them into it. Never have. Never will. The art attracts them. It is like magic, drawing the moth to the flame.'

'And you're the flame?' I replied, leading him into a trap of his own making.

His boastful smile made me want to throw something at him. 'As I said, the women come to me and they have no desire to leave. When I tire of them, they are sad, but grateful to have been able to spend the time they have had with me. They get to cherish that memory for the rest of their lives. Take Evelyn, for instance. Even though I tired of her, insisting we divorce so I could move on with my life, she remained by my side, finding a way that she could stay in my life by becoming my manager.'

August really was something else. I was certain I had never met anyone so in love with themselves. 'These moths, how often do they get burned?' His eyes narrowed. Not committing to an answer, he wanted to hear more from me. 'When I look, will I find that pushing out one woman to replace her with a younger one has always gone smoothly. Or have there been issues in the past?' A glance at Deepa Bhukari was all it took for her to have her tablet out. She would look for information on him, and if there was anything there, she would find it.

'No issues,' August spat. 'You want to know why Vanessa killed herself, well I can tell you that I have no idea. That she would take her own life is beyond my ability to understand.'

'Do you think that she might have been murdered?' I asked.

A muscle by his right eye twitched. It could mean something but might mean nothing. So too the bead of sweat which chose that moment to leave his hairline and trickle southward. I was making him uncomfortable, but I wasn't really getting anywhere.

I suspected him of knowing more than he was telling me, but did I suspect him of murder? No, not yet. I had no suspects. Nobody looked right for the crime so far, and I was constantly reminding myself that it was unprofessional to want him to be guilty.

He hadn't answered my question, but I wasn't going to say another word until he caved and spoke first. Just as I hoped, he could only stand the silent stares for so long. 'Who would want to kill her?' he asked, replying with a question rather than answering me.

'I was hoping you might tell me, August. Surely sleeping with her gave you some insight into her life.' I really wanted to hit him with questions about the other man in Vanessa's life, the mysterious B, but held off for now. Barbie would find a plethora of facts, maybe she would even track the mystery man down, or get through to him on his phone. If I returned in a few hours or at breakfast to hit August with more questions, I might by then know as much or possibly more than he did. That would swing the power balance in my direction. It was better to wait and come back stronger.

Pushing back my barstool, I said, 'Thank you for your time this evening, Mr Skies. I believe it will be necessary to ask you more questions later as our investigation develops.'

He tilted his head slightly. 'What exactly is it that you are investigating? What crime has been committed?'

Before answering, I took a second to assess the man sitting opposite me. He was utterly calm again, unconcerned that I might return to ask him more questions or that I was snooping around in the first place.

'I have reason to believe that Vanessa's death was staged to look like a suicide, Mr Skies. That being the case, she was murdered, and I intend to find out why and by whom.'

It was a bold statement, but if it worried him, he showed not the slightest trace of nervousness.

Turning away, I spoke to Lieutenant Bhukari, 'Can you please check to see if Scarlet is awake?' Better to send a woman into another woman's bedroom.

'Oh,' said Deepa. 'Dr Davis gave her a sedative at her request. He said she would be out of it for a couple of hours at least. I guess no one told you that.'

I said a bad word in my head. Scarlet found the body but that wasn't the only thing that made her interesting to talk to. She was the third woman in the love rectangle, and I wanted to know if she was Vanessa's friend or if the way Eoin described her was accurate. I didn't attempt to speak to her earlier because she was visibly upset, and because at the time we were looking at a suicide and had no reason to interview people. Now that I wanted to talk to her, I couldn't.

Moving away from August in the kitchen, the security officers followed me, I whispered, 'We've got no choice but to attempt the interviews in the morning instead. With Niamh inebriated and Scarlet drugged, we could come back in a couple of hours, but we might as well leave it until breakfast now.'

No one argued. They were probably grateful because it meant we could all get some sleep. The chaps in Vanessa's room were finished; there had been nothing to find. The oxycodone was already recorded as evidence, so too the champagne bottle and fingerprints had been taken from everyone who could be involved. There were people who were going to be busy tonight sifting and matching fingerprints, analysing the autopsy report and performing chemical analysis on the bathwater, but that didn't involve any of us, mercifully.

As a group, we left the Prestwick Suite, paused in the passageway outside to briefly discuss what we needed to do in the morning and went our separate ways. I said goodnight to Sam — he was going back to his parent's cabin, escorted there by the security team before they made their way down to their own accommodation at the bottom of the ship.

A History of Violence

I found Barbie and Jermaine still awake and working on Vanessa's secret phone. The dachshunds streaked across the carpet to get to me and I fussed them all, cooing nonsense at each in turn and scratching tummies.

Jermaine came to take my bag and coat. 'A night cap, madam?' he asked.

I could see an empty glass on the desk near Barbie. Condensation on the outside told me it was freshly finished. A cold gin sounded good, but I expected to be up early in the morning so I declined. 'No, thank you, Jermaine. I have a feeling this case is going to demand an early start. I still need to interview Niamh and Scarlet, and I'll probably need to reinterview everyone else.'

'You didn't get to speak with them yet?' Jermaine voiced his surprise.

Crossing the suite to get to Barbie, I revealed, 'Niamh's drunk. Because we started out viewing this as a suicide, I didn't think to lock them down. Had it been an obvious murder, I could have placed guards in their cabin and kept her sober. Too late now so I'll need to speak with her in the morning. I also figure we might know a little more by then. Scarlet was given a sedative by Dr Davis, which is unhelpful, but not his fault. Did you guys find anything? Were you able to speak with B?'

Barbie wasn't looking my way, but as I approached, she swivelled around on her chair to face me. 'We must have called that number fifty times or more.' She picked up the phone to check. 'I misspoke, it's only forty-eight times.' For good measure, she pressed the dial button again and switched it to speaker.

Just as before, it rang and rang until it switched to voicemail.

'We left messages,' Jermaine let me know, 'asking B to make contact. Nothing so far with that approach either.'

'As for the messages on the phone, it's just a lot more of the same. I think there was a whole load of conversation that took place before these messages start and the first one suggests she was using a different phone before.'

'They've never met though,' Jermaine clarified.

Barbie nodded, 'That's right. We couldn't find anything that says how they came to know each other, but my guess would still be internet dating or something like that.'

'Nothing about why she needs to escape August?' I asked. 'No accusations of abuse or suggestions that he might hurt her?'

I got a head shake this time. 'Nothing like that.' It was disappointing to hear. 'But,' Barbie added, 'I did find out that August was charged with causing bodily harm to a woman called Megan Flowers. He was found guilty and had to pay her compensation at a civil court.'

This was news. 'How long ago?'

'Seventeen years ago,' she replied immediately. 'I cannot be sure, but it looks as though this isn't the only incident.' She turned back to the computer, clicking a tab at the bottom of the page. 'Jermaine and I found newspaper articles where three other women came forward at the time of the court case to claim they had been threatened with harm if they left him. They were all former models of his, each then went silent.'

'Like he paid them off?' I guessed.

Barbie nodded, her eyes still on the screen which illuminated her face in the dimly lit space. 'That would be my guess. However, since he has this moneyless policy and won't sell his paintings, I wondered how he could have done so. It turns out he did sell some.'

I was at her shoulder now, looking at the same page of information as she brought up another tab. 'When?' I begged to know, my heart beating faster than normal now as I waited to hear the vital clue that would give me what I needed to nail him.

Barbie reached forward, extending a slender finger to point to a spot on the screen. 'Right around the same time.' I looked at the date of the article - it was seventeen years ago.

'He couldn't avoid dealing with the criminal charge and the civil lawsuit brought by Megan Flowers, but the other women were silenced with money.'

'And no doubt a gagging order enforced by lawyers,' said Jermaine.

'You've got names?'

Barbie nodded. 'They are named when they raise the accusations and talked about in articles that range over a six-month period. August Skies has some detractors in the press, but nothing really stuck.'

Leaning over to read the screen, I straightened again and started walking around the room as I let my brain connect the dots. 'He doesn't care about money, but he can't have his reputation marred by bad press that might impact the commissions because they allow him to live the way he does. A big part of his lifestyle is the hedonistic sleep-with-multiple-beautiful-young-women policy he somehow has despite being married. If the women such as Vanessa knew the truth, they would think twice about entering into a relationship with him.'

'Yet he continues to manipulate them.' Barbie pointed to the phone. 'These messages show that Vanessa wanted to escape from August, but something was holding her back and it was enough to make her want to keep the phone hidden so he wouldn't find out what she was planning.'

'He did find out though,' I said aloud, my eyes narrowing as I tried to assess the truth of that statement. Despite Dr Davis's tentative verdict of suicide, I remained convinced Vanessa had been murdered. Evelyn was in custody but was she guilty of anything? The note on her PDA was damning, but could August have put it there to throw us off his scent?

'Can we be sure, madam?' asked Jermaine. 'How could we prove he knew?'

I blew out a frustrated breath. It was the perfect question. We needed one decent piece of evidence. Something that would tie him to Vanessa's death. It could come in any shape and we were looking for it in many ways, but time was not our friend.

Barbie covered her mouth as a deep yawn gripped her. As it so often does, her yawn made Jermaine reveal his own fatigue. It was indication enough that the day was done. We could keep going slavishly but getting some sleep and tackling the problem with fresh eyes in the morning made more sense.

Five minutes later, I was crawling into bed with three sausage dogs arranging themselves on my duvet. It was pitch black in my bedroom even with the curtains open. It was one of the things I learned when I first came on board – how dark it is out on the ocean. If the moon is on the right side of the ship, I had light to see by, but when it wasn't, the superstructure cast a shadow that cut out all light.

Thinking I was too tired for it to matter if there was light or not, I let my head sink into my sumptuous pillow and was oblivious within seconds.

Little did I know how little sleep I would actually get.

Rude Awakening

I won't say that I am used to having my sleep disturbed but must admit it happens often enough that it no longer shocks me. As is often the case, it was the dogs that brought me from my slumber as they exploded in a fit of barking and ran across my bed. Georgie had been tucked into the gap under my arms and chose to run across my chest to get to the door as it opened.

Blearily trying to make out the time on the clock, I gave up and flicked on my bedside light.

Barbie was peering around the door. 'Are you awake, Patty?' she whispered.

Her attempt at being quiet made me chuckle at least. 'I am now. As if anyone could sleep through three dachshunds trying to kill an intruder.'

'Sorry. I had to wake you. There's been another murder. No question that it might be suicide this time.'

Instantly fully awake, I rubbed at my eyes and swung my legs over the side of the bed. The Dachshunds hadn't returned which meant they'd found something more interesting than sleep in the main area of the suite.

It turned out to be Lieutenant Baker. His uniform was fresh even if the man inside it looked less than raring to go. It had only been four hours since I last saw him, so he hadn't had much sleep. He was standing next to Jermaine who was dressed in navy blue silk pyjamas, a towelling robe and leather house slippers.

Baker got straight to the point. 'A patrol discovered blood leaking under a cabin door. They forced entry and discovered the two occupants had been brutally slain.' He paused for just a second to let that sink in. 'It was Eoin Planchet's cabin. He is dead. The other victim is Scarlet O'Reilly.'

My brow furrowed, unable to believe what I was hearing. It was like getting punched in the head and gut at the same time and it made my vision swim.

Both Jermaine and Lieutenant Baker stuck a hand out to steady me, grabbing my arms to stop me from falling. I wasn't going to actually keel over, but I had gone woozy for a moment. I had seen these people just a few hours ago, how were they now both dead?

Getting my heartbeat back under control, I had to confirm what Baker said. 'Scarlet and Eoin are both dead and Scarlet was in Eoin's cabin.'

'Yes,' Baker confirmed.

'In the middle of the night?' I questioned, still certain I was hearing it wrong.

'Yes. They were both naked,' Baker reported. 'I think we can assume they were sleeping together.'

I had to argue. 'But he didn't have anything good to say about her. He called her an evil cow.' My sense of reality was being shaken.

Barbie pointed out, 'That would be a great thing to say if he wanted us to believe they were not sleeping together.'

I frowned even harder, trying to make the facts as presented fit together in my head. 'So he makes out that he doesn't like her while secretly sleeping with her. His girlfriend is in the brig, but to him that's just an opportunity to spend the night with the younger woman.' I huffed a breath of disbelief. 'The question, of course, is who killed them?'

'Indeed, madam,' agreed my butler.

I locked eyes with Lieutenant Baker. 'Evelyn Skies is still in the brig, yes?'

'Yes.'

'She's not guilty of killing Eoin and Scarlet,' I stated the obvious. 'That's not conclusive proof that she didn't kill Vanessa, but I'd be willing to bet money on it. How were they killed?' I asked.

'Stabbed,' Lieutenant Baker supplied without needing to think. 'There's no sign of the murder weapon. Not so far ...'

'But we're on a cruise ship with ocean all around us,' Barbie finished what the man in uniform was probably going to say.

Baker nodded. 'The knife used could easily have gone overboard.' I could see he was thinking something, and he started talking again before I needed to prompt him. 'The wounds are odd.'

In response, I started backing away, 'I need to get dressed,' I announced. 'Keep talking though.'

Barbie had on loose-fitting gym clothes, probably snagged on her way to see who was at the door, but said she was getting changed too.

I went into my bedroom, then reversed direction to stick my head back outside. 'Jermaine, sweetie. You should get back to bed. There's no telling what today might bring but we ought to be driving home later and at least one of us needs to be awake for it.'

'Very good, madam.'

In my bedroom, I threw the wardrobe doors open and wondered what I owned that could just be thrown on without looking like I had just thrown it on. Outside, Lieutenant Baker continued to tell me about the stab wounds, his voice carrying through the open door.

'The shape isn't like a normal stab wound.' He was speaking slowly, struggling to find the words he wanted.

'How so?' I asked, questioning whether I could get away with a hat instead of dealing with my bed hair.

'Well … the wounds are long, but thin. I can't picture what kind of knife might have made them. Normally, if the blade is deep from edge to edge, it also must be wide across the cross section, otherwise it will bend or snap. This is neither. Also, it is double edged … sort of.'

'Sort of?' I hurriedly swiped on some colour around my eyes, trying to hide the bags I could see.

Baker's voice drifted in through my open bedroom door again. 'It will be easier to show you.'

I huffed out a breath, muttering, 'So much to look forward to.'

'Sorry, I didn't catch that.'

'Nothing important,' I assured the lieutenant as I rejoined him. Barbie came hopping from her own bedroom, one running shoe on and the other being slid into place. With both on, she grinned at us and jogged on the spot energetically.

'Nothing like a little exercise to wake a person up, eh?' It made me feel tired just watching her.

With a sigh and using the back of my hand to stifle a yawn, I said, 'Let's get it done.'

Unpleasant Scene

I see way too many bodies. None would be a nice number. That's how many bodies I want to see from now on. I'm not going to describe the scene to you because then it will be in your head too. Let's just say it wasn't very nice and leave it at that.

The victims were both naked, just as Lieutenant Baker described. Eoin was by the door; it was his blood that leaked under it to be spotted by a patrol going past. Scarlet was in the bedroom, lying half on and half off the bed, her eyes locked on nothing as they stared to the ceiling.

I took in as much detail as I thought necessary as quickly as I could and then went back out to the passageway for some air. Barbie hadn't come in, remaining outside when I begged her to save herself from seeing things which could never be erased.

Inside the cabin, members of the security team were working. They didn't say much, going about their assigned or assumed tasks with ruthless efficiency because none of them wanted to be involved in this side of their job.

Dr Davis arrived, roused from his bed if the creases in his face were any indication. The man looked tired and his presence, required so that death could be officially recorded, was a nonsense to my mind – the victims were as dead as could be.

I got a nod from him as he went by me and into the cabin.

'Is it awful?' Barbie asked me, her voice barely audible despite the silence in the passageway.

To avoid giving her any kind of description, I gritted my teeth and said, 'I want to know why they are dead.'

It didn't make sense, that was my biggest issue. Vanessa being murdered by August I could figure out. I couldn't prove it yet. In fact, I didn't have a shred of evidence, yet I was convinced he was guilty. His young lover was choosing to leave him and somehow he'd found out about it. He saw it as an insult, an afront to the image he had of himself as the great man, so he'd killed her and made it look like Evelyn did it.

I explained my thoughts to Barbie, both of us talking in hushed whispers no one could hear. She listened to what I had to say before speaking.

'I guess that makes sense, Patty. I don't recall when you were ever wrong.'

That was nice of her to say but it didn't get me anywhere. 'If we accept that August killed Vanessa, why are Eoin and Scarlet dead? Because they were lovers and August couldn't stand the insult?'

Barbie shrugged. 'Possibly. If August really did kill Vanessa, then it stands to reason that he also killed Scarlet. Perhaps he had to kill Eoin to get to her.'

'August isn't exactly young and fit to be taking on Eoin the giant bodybuilder,' I countered.

Barbie looked down at the unpleasant dark stain on the passageway carpet. 'Maybe he didn't have to. August knocks on the door, Eoin opens it, and August stabs him. Before Eoin even registers who is outside, he is fighting for his life.'

I wriggled my lips around, trying on the scenario for size. 'Who answers the door naked?'

Barbie hadn't thought of that. 'Could it be that August stripped him after he stabbed him?'

It wasn't impossible. It didn't feel right though. Something felt off. 'I need to speak to Evelyn again.' My announcement was made too quietly for Lieutenant Baker to hear, yet he chose that moment to poke his head out of the cabin.

'I need to break the news to the passengers travelling with them. I'm going to start with Evelyn Skies. Do you want to come, Mrs Fisher?'

Want would not be the word I would choose, but I was going anyway.

I was surprised to find Lieutenant Rudman still behind the desk in the brig.

She chuckled when I asked her about it. 'It's a twelve-hour shift. I just got started a few minutes before you arrived yesterday. I like the night shifts anyway.' She held up a thick book. 'Less happens, and I'm studying for my engineering exam.'

'You plan to stay with Purple Star?' I asked.

She nodded. 'I like travelling. I'm married to a chef; we met on board. There are always positions open for engineers. It's one of the easiest routes to get to the top, so to speak. Not that I got much done last night.'

'Oh, really,' I replied, showing interest to be polite.

'The prisoner's phone would not stop ringing. It went on for hours. I kept hoping it would go to voicemail because maybe that would be the end of it, but it must have rung off forty times before someone did leave a message and then it was just some guy with an upper-crust English accent. He sounded like the fella that does the talking clock.'

I heard what Lieutenant Rudman was telling me, but I wasn't really listening, I was itching to get on with the next step.

Lieutenant Baker was dealing with one of Rudman's colleagues, arranging for Evelyn Skies to be brought from her cell to an interview room. I felt terrible for her. As far as I was concerned, she was innocent and should not be in here. Now, we had to tell her that her boyfriend was not only dead but had been cheating on her with another woman. Had she not been incarcerated the murder might not have happened. Or, on the flip side, she might have ended up dead too.

The one thing I could be sure of was her lack of involvement in the latest murders. According to Dr Davis, they had died between two thirty and three this morning, a narrow window he could determine from the level of morbidity and their retained body temperature. The things I have learned in the last six months needed to come with an erase button.

When she was ready, Lieutenant Baker got the nod, but as we were about to go through to speak to her, Lieutenant Rudman stopped me.

'I don't know if this is in any way pertinent,' she started. 'I had to supervise Mrs Skies surrendering her clothing and there are several bruises on her body that ...' she paused, moving her lips around as she sought the right words. 'It looks to me like she has an abusive boyfriend. I remember seeing other women with similar marks. I asked her about it, but she said she fell down the stairs at home last week and it's all from that.'

I logged the information, thanking Rudman for revealing what she knew, and we went through to find Evelyn. Back in interview room two where we last spoke to her the previous evening, she was behind the desk yet again with two members of the security team watching her from either side of the door.

Acting in his official capacity, since I as yet have none, Lieutenant Baker broke the news of Eoin Planchet's death.

Evelyn didn't react at all for a couple of seconds. Then abruptly she started to hyperventilate. The colour drained from her skin and her eyes widened as panic gripped her. Seeing her distress made me want to go to her and it was a good thing I did as she fainted just as I got to my feet.

I had to lunge forward, putting my hands out to arrest her fall which at least stopped her head from bouncing off the table as she slid to the deck.

Baker moved fast too, coming to her aid but she was coming around again by the time he knelt by her side. An awful keening noise filled the room as the poor woman folded into a ball and sobbed her grief.

It was ten minutes before we could get any sense from her, most of which I spent kneeling on the cold steel deck holding her hand and making soothing sounds. I found there were no words of comfort I could offer. She was in the brig because a woman had died, and she was found with evidence suggesting she was responsible. More than ever, I felt convinced the evidence had been planted.

Once Evelyn was sufficiently recovered and back in her chair, I tugged at Lieutenant Baker's arm and got him to come with me to the passageway outside. 'The chaps going through all the physical evidence, they checked for fingerprints on the PDA, right?'

'They had a whole heap of items to go through, Mrs Fisher, and not a lot of time since we gave it all to them. It'll be the same team that are upstairs now dealing with the mess of Eoin and Scarlet.'

The pressure of time was upon us for sure. 'Can you check, please? That poor woman is in here and having to deal with her grief alone because of a single piece of evidence we found on her PDA.'

Lieutenant Baker wasn't arguing, he had his radio out and ready to make the call, but had to say, 'By her own admission, she couldn't think of anyone who could have put the note on it and claimed she rarely, if ever, lets it out of her sight.'

I didn't respond, letting him make the call to see what had been found. I felt like crossing my fingers and hoping.

A tired sounding woman identifying herself as Rodriguez answered his question. 'Lots of partials, some of which were probably not those of Mrs

Skies, but nothing we could identify as belonging to another member of her party.'

Baker glanced my way, his expression asking me what I wanted to do.

'Ask her to check again. She needs to be more thorough. It could be the difference between catching the killer or not.' I could see Lieutenant Baker didn't like having to pass along that instruction, but he did it, adding work to a person who already sounded like she had too much and messing with her order of priority. I hoped she would give it her full attention because I doubted she believed it was necessary.

Going back into the interview room, Evelyn was terribly tearful but more composed than before. Lieutenant Rudman arrived with a cup of tea for her.

'Thank you,' she accepted it gratefully. 'That was quite a shock,' she murmured. 'Do you know who killed him?'

I shook my head as I retook my seat. 'I'm afraid not. Actually, I'm here in the hope you can shed some light on what has been happening.'

Her blank expression encouraged me to press on.

'What was Eoin's opinion of Scarlet?' I posed the question and fell silent, wondering what she might say.

Her face suggested she found the question surprising and she looked at me for a full five seconds before she gasped. 'Did she kill him! Is that what happened?'

I repeated my question. 'What was Eoin's opinion of Scarlet. Did he ever talk about her?'

Evelyn was holding her head with one hand, cradling the left side of her face with shaky fingers. 'He … he never really spoke about her. I guess I caught him looking at her once or twice, but that's just what men do. She was young and very pretty.'

'When I spoke to him yesterday, he called her an evil cow. Why would he do that?' My question didn't shock her. There was no sudden jerk of her head at my words which meant she already knew what he thought and was lying about it.

'Sorry,' she replied with a half-hearted shrug, her head and eyes fixed firmly on the surface of the table between us. 'I lied then.' She huffed and fidgeted. 'I thought they might be having an affair,' she finally admitted. 'I wasn't sure. I hadn't confronted him about it, but I walked in on them talking once or twice and they would immediately stop talking. They would be standing a little too close to each other and feel the need to step apart when they saw me.'

I kept silent, waiting to see if she would have even more to say. Her eyes came up to meet mine, her lips trembling and tears still flowing. 'Is that why he was killed? Did August do it?'

'Would August kill him?' I posed a leading question.

Evelyn bit her lip before whispering, 'August could get very jealous. He wanted things to be the way he wanted them to be. He hurt me once … I threatened to leave him, and he went berserk. I thought he was going to kill me. I had to have one of my teeth capped from where he hit me. If he found out Scarlet was having an affair with Eoin, he might hurt them both. Where is Scarlet now?'

I drew in a deep breath, exchanged a glance with Lieutenant Baker and let him deliver the news.

Evelyn was rightly shocked. Two people had been brutally murdered and the inescapable conclusion was that Eoin and Scarlet were lovers.

'Will you release me now?' Evelyn wanted to know.

I wanted to, but I knew Lieutenant Baker would argue. The evidence against her demanded she be retained in custody until it could conclusively be discounted. I had no idea when that might occur but worried she would be transferred into police custody in a few hours. Once she was out of my hands, she would have to start the process of proving her innocence all over again.

For her sake, as well as for my own good conscience, I needed to solve this case fast.

Baker and I left Evelyn with the officers assigned to the brig. She was to be escorted back to her cell where a chaplain of her choice would be sent to speak with her and offer spiritual guidance. I couldn't help her with her grief, that's not within my set of skills. What I could do was catch August and in doing so, set the poor woman free.

Accusations

Lieutenant Baker looked alarmed when I started to hammer on the door to the Prestwick Suite. I thought he was going to try to stop me, but his half-raised arms dropped back to his sides when he saw my expression.

I'd sent Barbie back to our suite and told her to get some sleep. We would all benefit from more sleep, so though it wasn't an option for me to get any, I saw no reason to keep her up.

'If you're sure, Patty,' she'd replied around a yawn, wanting to go, but not wanting to leave my side.

'It will be dawn in another hour or so at which point there will be breakfast hopefully. I'll see you then.' My reply hosted no discussion on the subject.

I hammered again and honestly thought about kicking the door. August was guilty of three murders; of that I was certain. I just had to prove it and I was going to start by making him feel uncomfortable.

Just as I was going to shout through the door, the sound of it being unlocked gave me reason to pause. The suite's butler, a Frenchman named Gerard stood inside. He bore a haughty expression despite wearing night clothes, his usually waxed moustache not quite straight where he'd been sleeping on it.

'Yes?' he replied, blocking our entrance with his body. 'Can I 'elp you?'

I didn't get to snap the snarky remark forming on my lips because Lieutenant Baker pushed by him, forcing the Frenchman to step aside as he barrelled in.

'Ship's business,' was all Baker said. Once we were inside and the butler had the door closed again, he issued an order. 'Wake Mr and Mrs Skies. Tell them security are waiting for them.'

Gerard looked as if he might argue for a moment but settled for glaring at both of us for a second before crossing the suite to knock politely on the door to the master bedroom.

Once he was out of sight, Baker turned to me. 'Mrs Fisher I must insist that you allow me to report the deaths before you say anything. I know you believe Mr Skies is guilty, but until we have something to tie him to the crime, we have to assume they are not aware, and announce the deaths in a dignified way.'

Any argument I might have wanted to present went out of the window when August burst from his bedroom.

'What is the meaning of this!' he bellowed, anger making his head the shade of a raspberry. 'Constant disturbances yesterday, and now you wake me in the middle of the night!'

'It's six in the morning,' I pointed out.

Lieutenant Baker shot me a pleading look, stopping me before I could say anything else. August was winding up to deliver a fresh tirade of unpleasantness, when the man in uniform interrupted him.

'Mr Skies, I am afraid I am here to deliver terrible news.' The simple opening statement stopped August in his tracks just as his wife, Niamh, emerged from the bedroom behind him looking exhausted and rather haggard from her overindulgence the previous evening.

'What is it?' she asked, her voice full of trepidation.

Lieutenant Baker did his best to stand upright and appear professional while delivering the news of the two murders. Unsure what reaction to expect, I was watching August when I should have had my eyes on Niamh.

From the corner of my eye, I spotted her looking at August. I missed her expression, and when I turned my gaze on her, Niamh's face was set as neutrally as she could manage.

'This is ridiculous,' growled August.

'I am sorry for your loss,' Lieutenant Baker repeated. 'Perhaps you would like to take a seat so you can let the information settle in. I'm sure this must be quite a shock.'

August frowned as if he'd just been handed soiled underwear with a request to eat it. 'Quite a shock? Quite a shock?' he repeated. 'I'm on an around the world cruise to paint a series of inspiring seascapes and in less than twenty-four hours both my muses have been killed. Quite a shock, the man says. Tell me this,' he wagged a finger at Baker, 'how am I supposed to paint now?'

My eyebrows flared. Three people were dead, and his only concern was the inspiration for his paintings.

'Can you account for your time between midnight last night and now, Mr Skies?' I asked, a hard edge to my voice.

August narrowed his eyes at me, and his lips took on a nasty curl. One foot stepped forward, his muscles tensing, and I think he would have hit me if Lieutenant Baker hadn't spoken.

'We need to eliminate you from our enquiries, Mr Skies,' Baker told him, drawing his attention away from me.

Niamh flopped onto a couch and pulled her feet up so they were under her body. She looked terrible. 'God, my head is pounding,' she muttered, holding it with one hand. 'I'll never touch another drop, I swear.'

It had been a long time since I'd suffered a hangover, but there must be very few people on the planet who do not know what it is like to have overindulged. Before anyone could say anything, she bolted from the couch, flying back to her bedroom while holding a hand over her mouth – she was going to be sick.

Mercifully, she kicked the bedroom door shut behind her and the sound of yesterday's meals returning didn't reach our ears.

With her gone, it left August standing by himself in the middle of his suite's living space. He was fuming, his rage apparent, but he'd not answered my question yet.

I prompted him. 'Can you account for your whereabouts since we left your suite last night, Mr Skies. Three people connected to you are dead, and you have more motive than most to want them that way.'

When he turned his eyes on me, the artists glare could have cut through steel. 'What possible motive could I have for wanting any of them dead?' he demanded I explain.

I held his gaze when I said, 'Megan Flowers.'

He must have been expecting me to say something else, because my response caught him off guard. 'What?' he replied, startled by the name from his past.

I repeated it, this time letting a smile curl the corners of my mouth. 'Megan Flowers. She filed a criminal case against you when you hit her, and then won a civil lawsuit that opened a small floodgate for other women to claim they had suffered the same at your hands. Is that ringing any bells?'

'I was innocent of all charges,' he snarled, his anger doubling at being forced to relive the memory.

'Is that why you paid them off?' I challenged him. 'Because you were innocent? You had to sell some of your paintings to make them go away, didn't you?'

The same tick I saw yesterday twitched again now. Beneath the skin above his left eye, a muscle spasmed as he tried to maintain control. 'That had nothing to do with anything that has happened here,' he managed through clenched teeth.

I made a show of raising my eyebrows. 'Really? You see, I think it has everything to do with it. You have a history of trying to control the women in your life and you have shown me that you believe yourself to be God's gift to them. Why would they ever leave you? Isn't that what you asked me? But they do try to leave you, don't they? You lure them in, but when they want to leave, you threaten them, and if they persist, you hurt them. Don't you, August?'

He said nothing, glowering with eyes that spoke of terrible things if he were ever to get me alone.

I nodded to myself and defeated his gaze by taking my eyes away, pacing around the room as I talked. 'You found out that Vanessa had fallen in love with someone else. You couldn't stand the insult to your ego that her choosing to leave you presented so you got her drunk and gave her drugs and then you killed her in her bath, making it look like a suicide.'

'Or it was just a suicide,' he countered, doing nothing to hide the malice in his voice.

Unperturbed by his response, I said, 'You were worried someone might question the evidence so you laid a dummy trail leading back to your ex-wife. You knew Vanessa had been sneaking off to see Eoin, so why not make Evelyn out to be driven crazy by jealousy, just the way you were. You put a note on her PDA, confident we would find it if we ever looked. That might have worked if you hadn't then killed your next two victims while she was locked away in the brig.'

'I haven't killed anyone,' August growled. 'I was in bed with my wife all night. I am certain she will confirm that when you ask her.'

I thought it quite telling that he hadn't thought to check if his sick wife were all right in their bedroom. Having dashed away to vomit, surely a husband, even one conducting multiple affairs under his wife's nose, would know to show a little concern.

Continuing to accuse him, I wagged a finger at him from across the room. 'You found out about Scarlet sleeping with Eoin. It made your blood boil, didn't it, August?' I was goading him, pushing his buttons in the hope I could get him to tip his hand. Angry people say all manner of things they later regret. 'How did you do it, August? Did you stab Eoin the moment he opened the door?'

I swung my face to look right at him; would he betray the truth in his eyes?

Expecting to see him seething as I laid bare his carefully constructed murder, it was my turn to be caught out because he chose to smile at me instead. A snort of amusement left him as his grin widened.

'You don't have a scrap of evidence, do you?' he stated, the concept amusing to him. 'You think I did it, but you can't prove a thing, so you came here hoping to rile me up into admitting to something I haven't done.'

'Where were you last night?' I asked again.

His smile widened yet further. 'In bed with my wife, Mrs Fisher. She will claim the same and there isn't a thing you can do to prove otherwise, or you would have done so already.'

Now my teeth were clenched. I had just taken down one of the largest ... possibly the largest criminal organisation on the planet, yet I was being thwarted by a narcissistic artist from Ireland. What was wrong with me? I am better than this, but I was playing into his hands. It was like trying to bluff at poker when he had already seen my cards.

I didn't like it, not one bit, but I was holding a losing hand and the only thing I could do was fold.

'I need to speak with your wife,' I managed to say.

He grinned at me once more, the small snort of amusement accompanied this time by a waggle of his eyebrows. I was a clown to him. 'I'll just get her,' he promised, heading for the bedroom door.

He was in their bedroom longer than the task required, but I had to consider that Niamh might still be vomiting, or that he might be having trouble coaxing her into coming out again. I made to move toward the bedroom door, intending to see what the hold up was and wondering if I might find him hiding the murder weapon or acting in a manner that might suggest his guilt.

Lieutenant Baker caught my arm at the elbow and held me back. 'Please, Mrs Fisher,' he insisted.

Frowning at him, but keeping my mouth shut for now, I waited. August reappeared a few seconds later, swiftly followed by Niamh, though swiftly might not be the right word given how slowly she was moving. She paused in the bedroom doorway, holding onto the door and the frame as if they were keeping her upright. She looked washed out; exhausted from poor quality sleep and poisoned by the amount of alcohol she'd foolishly drunk.

There was a tone of derision in August's voice when he said, 'It's amateur sleuth hour, Niamh. Do you think you can answer a few questions for Mrs Fisher?' Turning to look at me, he added, 'Please don't bore her for too long, Mrs Fisher, I think she could do with some more rest. If there's nothing else …'

When neither Lieutenant Baker nor I attempted to stop him, he took it as freedom to do as he pleased. Passing his wife in the bedroom doorway, he went inside and shut the door.

'What is it you want to know?' Niamh Skies asked, letting go of the doorframe and taking a shaky step forward. The nearest couch was six feet away and she made a very slow beeline for it, walking with her arms out slightly for balance. She stank of whiskey, not that I was going to mention it, but I had to wonder how much she drank yesterday. She'd seemed shaken by the news of Vanessa's apparent suicide, but it never once occurred to me that she would do this to herself.

Once she was sitting, I aimed my own derriere into one corner of the couch opposite and, in a kind, soft voice asked her, 'Has August ever hurt you?'

Her eyes snapped up, a reaction she instantly regretted for the wave of nausea it brought. Slowly settling back into the couch with her eyes closed, she replied, 'I've no wish to discuss the subject, Mrs Fisher.'

'It may be pertinent to the …'

She cut me off hard by saying. 'No.'

Unsure what she meant, I tried to clarify, 'No, he's never hurt you?'

'No, Mrs Fisher, I will not discuss the subject. What else would you like to know?'

Feeling a little flummoxed, I tried a different approach. 'Did you know Scarlet and Eoin were lovers?'

Her head was back, and her eyes were closed; the one position she felt like she might not throw up again. 'I suspected,' she admitted. 'Little things gave them away.'

'Like what?' I pushed for more.

'They were furtive around one another. Eoin actively avoided her when he could.' She thought for a moment. 'I think the biggest clue was when I noticed the scent of his aftershave on one of her jackets. I found it on the floor next to the stairs at our home outside Dublin. I think she'd hung it on the end of the banister and either missed or it got knocked off. Either way, when I picked it up, I could smell him.'

Eoin fooled me completely yesterday. I would have testified that he hated the young woman though I wouldn't have been able to say why. He didn't though, he was sleeping with her and doing his best to make sure no one knew.

Worrying that my detective abilities were leaving me, I pressed on. 'Did you say anything to August?'

'Ha! Goodness, no.' Niamh replied in an instant. Then she saw the trap I'd walked her into. 'You are about to ask me why not, and I will have to say because he would have gotten angry. Very clever, Mrs Fisher. August is a jealous man. He always has been. He could never handle his women wanting to end their relationships with him. That doesn't make him a killer.'

'Can you account for his whereabouts last night?' I asked.

'He was in bed with me all night, Mrs Fisher.'

It was the answer I expected, and my response was already on the tip of my tongue. 'How can you be sure, Mrs Skies? You were so inebriated last night, you had to be carried to bed.'

Niamh cracked one eyelid, examining me carefully through the narrow slit without moving her head. 'He woke me to check I was alright when he came to bed. That was just a few minutes after midnight. It was also when I started being sick, I'm ashamed to admit. I wasn't able to go back to sleep and spent most of the last six hours going back and forth to the bathroom. August was in bed, snoring quietly the whole time.'

Now I was getting mad. I was certain she was lying, covering for her husband, and helping him get away with murder. Was it because she was in on it? She was too drunk to have played a part in the killing, but if she was lying now then she was complicit.

'Did you also know Vanessa was leaving?' I changed tack again. My question caused a faint movement of her head and both eyes came open. She was checking to see if I was being truthful. 'We found a secret phone she'd kept hidden for fear August would discover it and learn of her plan.'

Carefully, in deference to her hangover and delicate state, she tilted her head so she was looking directly at me. 'You're serious.'

'Yes. Did he know?'

She shook her head in wonder. 'He never said anything if he did. No,' she blurted. 'No, he couldn't have.'

'Why?' I demanded. 'Because he would have hurt her if he so much as suspected?'

From the look on her face, I'd given Niamh something to think about. Becoming conscious that I was watching her, she closed her eyes again and let her head fall slowly backward until it met the couch.

'I really don't feel well, Mrs Fisher. Can we continue this another time when I am more rested?'

I was about to say no when Lieutenant Baker got to his feet. 'Of course, Mrs Skies. Thank you for your time. We hope you feel better soon.'

I leapt to my feet and grabbed Baker's sleeve. 'What are you doing?' I hissed. 'We need to press them until one of them slips up.'

He gave a determined shake of his head, ducking his head to whisper in my ear, 'We have nothing on them. If we keep pressing, we are in danger of embarrassing the cruise line and that will cost me my job. If we find evidence that links Mr Skies to either crime, then we can come back and try again.'

I didn't like it. Not one bit, but I was getting nowhere and that was all because the only thing tying August to the murders was my belief that he was guilty.

Gerard, the French butler had already positioned himself by the door to see us out. It seemed everyone was ready to put me back in my place.

Well, I might be leaving with my tail between my legs, but I wasn't done yet. Not by a long shot.

Fighting with a Friend

In the passageway outside, I took a pause and gathered myself.

Lieutenant Baker said, 'That could have gone better.'

'Did we really have to cut it short like that?' I tried to not snap at him.

'We cannot accuse passengers without just cause, Mrs Fisher. It's that simple.'

He was sailing close to the point where he would be talking down to me and it came on top of August laughing at me and Niamh dismissing me. It was too much. 'No wonder you never solve any crimes without my help,' I snapped. 'All this tiptoeing around when anyone can see the man has murdered three people since coming on the ship yesterday.'

Now that I was on the attack, my friend, Lieutenant Baker, responded in kind. 'No one can see it, Mrs Fisher! That's the point. You don't have a shred of evidence. You may be a top-drawer detective, but you've lost the plot on this one. Innocent until proven guilty. All you have are a few wild guesses. Dr Davis is still claiming Vanessa's death was most likely suicide and you've yet to demonstrate that it wasn't.'

'Oh, open your eyes, man!' I raged, fatigue, frustration, and shame because he was at least partly right, all welling up to burst from me like a volcano blowing its top. 'August Skies is going to get away with three murders because no one but me is willing to do what it takes to catch him!'

Lieutenant Baker bit down his next words and took a breath to calm himself. 'Mrs Fisher, I must caution you against acting unlawfully in your pursuit of Mr Skies. Until Purple Star officially appoints you, you are a consultant assisting our investigation. If you can produce evidence that unequivocally points to August's involvement in the murders, I will act. Until then, I must insist that you take it down a notch.'

I breathed in and out a few times, keeping my mouth shut for fear of what might come out if I opened it. When I was calm, I said, 'Expect to hear from me soon.'

Because I was upset and didn't want to be arguing with a person I had great warmth and respect for, I turned about without another word and walked away. The door to my suite was just a few yards away and I got through it before the need to cry overcame me.

I'm not the sort of woman who cries a lot. I cried the day I discovered Charlie had been cheating on me, and I cried when Mr Worthington of Worthington, Worthington, Worthington, and Smythe took me to the house the Maharaja of Zangrabar had chosen to gift me. On that occasion it was Jermaine stepping from the house to fill my heart with joy that caused my tears. I was fighting them back now because my life was a rollercoaster that never seemed to stop, and I wanted to get off for a while.

Inside the door of my suite, the dogs rushed me, and Jermaine appeared as he always does. Fitted out in his full butler's uniform, complete with white gloves, he took one look at my face and was not surprised when I threw my arms around him. I needed someone to hug.

Uncertainty about the impending divorce, the pressure of the Godmother's terror finally receding like a pressure cap suddenly removed, the fight with Baker, all backed by frustration over this case and constantly questioning if I was right to upend my life to move in with Alistair had all combined to overwhelm me.

Jermaine held me for more than a minute while I let a few tears fall and tried to straighten out my brain.

The ship's mighty engines shut off; the change only noticeable because the distant background rumble was suddenly absent. We were back in Southampton. If I wanted to, I could disembark and forget all about August Skies. Alistair and I, together with Barbie and Jermaine, Sam and his parents, and Mike Atwell, could travel in convoy back to East Malling where tonight we could have dinner in our own houses.

I cannot claim that I wasn't tempted to do exactly that. The comfort and security of my own house, in my home village. The opportunity to show Alistair where I grew up and now live. I had to go anyway, but could I really just walk away from this case? August was guilty, and if I could just get my brain up to speed, I would work out how he'd done it and find the evidence to convict him.

Just as I broke away from Jermaine, placing a hand on his chest and patting him in thanks rather than speak in case my voice cracked, Barbie came out of her bedroom.

'Hey, guys?' she hallooed, her expression becoming curious as she took in the way we were standing and wondered what she had interrupted. 'Everything okay?'

She was dressed for exercise and in that instant, the thing I wanted more than anything was to burn off some energy. Not that I was feeling energetic, you understand, but the pain of hard physical exertion would distract me for a while and wake me up, just as she claimed a few hours ago.

'Going to the gym?' I asked.

'Yeah?' she replied cautiously, framing it as a question because she wasn't sure why I was asking.

'Good. I'm coming too.'

Having been awake for more hours than was decent in the last twenty-four, I was hungry, my body thinking I should eat breakfast early just because I had been up for hours. Exercise would shut my stomach up for a while and let me eat at a more sensible time of the day. Jermaine offered to walk the dogs while we were at the gym, but Barbie had a better idea – shuttle sprints on the deck.

'It's about five degrees centigrade outside,' I pointed out, now wearing my super supportive Lycra and running shoes.

'Best you run fast then,' she countered, and leaving no chance for discussion, clapped her hands to get the dogs moving and ran for the door with all three chasing her.

Thinking I should have chosen clothes that covered my skin instead of three-quarter-length skin-tight shorts and a vest, I ran after her.

I knew she was right, and we would survive the cold air because we would be warmed by the exercise, but it was still jolly cold outside. The dogs didn't seem to care, running and barking and being generally excited as they followed Barbie and me up and down the deck.

We had the space to ourselves, no one else on board crazy enough to venture outside at this time or in this climate. That is until a couple, also dressed for running, pushed a door open and started to step outside.

Hyped up by the humans sprinting back and forth and Barbie's constant shouts of encouragement, all three dogs heard the new people at the same time and flew in their direction like three ankle height terror sausages.

Astonished by the noise, the man threw his weight backward through the still open door, shunting his wife/girlfriend and knocking her over in his haste to escape death by dachshund.

Defeated, the three dogs took to jumping on each other in a display of puppy-like wrestling. Two heads appeared at the window set into the door, looking down to see what it was that had just tried to kill them.

I waved and tried to gulp in enough air to say, 'Sorry,' but it came out with no volume due to my breathlessness.

Barbie laughed at me. 'Had enough?' she asked.

It was usually a trick question that led neatly into her stopping what we were doing so we could do something far more strenuous instead.

In a gasping rasp, I said, 'Never! Let's do more.'

It made her laugh at least. 'I think that will about do it,' she replied, starting to stretch in place. The dogs got scooped so the couple could come onto the deck without fear of arterial bleeding from their ankles, and we went back to the suite where a big surprise was waiting.

Fond Farewell

'Surprise!'

The shout from a dozen voices made me jump, my heart stopping and threatening to go on strike. I won't dwell on the fact that I almost wet myself.

It also shocked the dogs who responded by flying into the suite to attack the people waiting inside. I had to shout for them to desist but the people inside were familiar with the dopey sausages so simply picked them up when they tried to attack.

'What's going on?' I gasped. Still recovering from all the running around and the cold, I was short of breath and imagined I must look a terrible state.

In front of me as I looked into the suite were Rick and Akamu, Mavis and Agnes, Mike Atwell, Sam and his parents Melissa and Paul, plus Jermaine standing to one side of them all.

Alistair was nearest to me. 'Dinner was called abruptly to a halt last night,' he explained. 'That was supposed to be the chance for everyone to get together and say their farewells. Since that didn't happen, I invited everyone along for breakfast this morning.'

I smiled and felt my heart lift. These were my friends. Good people without whom I might not now be alive.

'Where's Lady Mary?' I asked, naming my socialite friend who appeared to be absent, but could be behind everyone sneaking in a cheeky gin and tonic before breakfast.

Alistair urged me to come into the suite. 'She sent her apologies. She had to leave early to meet with her husband. Her helicopter picked her up hours ago.'

'Thank you, everyone, this is wonderful. I, ah … I need to get a shower.'

Rick, in his usual manner agreed with me. 'You sure do, Patty. I can smell you from here.'

Both Mavis and Agnes slapped the back of his head, causing him to duck away and rub where it hurt.

Alistair smiled, and with an arm out to guide me, he ushered me to my bedroom. 'Take your time, Patricia, we will be waiting when you are ready.'

All notion of fatigue had left me. Well, except the muscular fatigue I now felt in my aching, wobbly legs. I didn't take my time; it felt impolite to do so though I was sure my friends were all chatting and feeling quite relaxed.

After a hurried shower and some swift dressing, a swipe of makeup finished the transformation from sweaty beast back into middle-aged woman and I felt ready to face the world. My friends were indeed relaxing in my suite. Some lounged on the couches drinking tea or coffee, others had drifted through to the kitchen area where I found Alistair and Jermaine making breakfast.

That Jermaine had accepted help was a mark of his respect for the captain; he'd never let me do anything and generally chased me away if I so much as tried to peel a banana. The room was filled with the smells of breakfast: freshly squeezed orange juice and coffee, toast, bacon, and a trace of vanilla coming from the waffle maker.

The dining table, which could be extended, was stretched out to fit all twelve of us. As I noted the dozen settings, I glanced back at Jermaine, this time realising he was out of his butler's uniform and wearing normal person clothes. We were leaving soon, and he was ready for the trip.

It made me smile to see him relaxing – it was something he did so rarely.

Barbie came to stand by my side. 'How are you feeling?' she asked. I knew the question wasn't one about my physical wellbeing after the tough workout, she was asking about my emotions.

'I think I might find it quite strange being on board and not living here in this suite,' I commented, my voice tinged with a little sadness, but also a trace of mirth for how insignificant of a concern it was.

'Me too,' said Barbie. 'It's been nice. You, me, and Jermaine ... like a little family. I'll miss that.'

The men were starting to serve breakfast, heaping platters of food being carried from the kitchen area to the dining table. The dogs, all three of them driven crazy by the smell of bacon and the abundant choice of people to fuss them, were whizzing around the room. I could see the potential of a spilled platter when they 'accidentally' tripped someone, but when my feet started on an intercept course to avert disaster, they stopped because Barbie appeared to have frozen.

She had a faraway look on her face, and her forehead was wrinkled as if thinking deep thoughts.

I called to the dogs, then turned my attention back to my blonde friend. 'What'cha doing?' I asked, grinning at her as she stared into space, transfixed by something in her head.

The spell broke, her eyes returning to the present. 'Sorry, we should join the others.' She looked down at the dogs, who had skidded to a stop by our feet and dropped into a crouch to scoop Smokey. 'I think someone needs a special hug.' she squished the boy dog under her chin. 'You're going home soon, sweetie,' she cooed in his ear. 'Your mummy will be so excited to see you.'

Barbie went by me to get to the breakfast bar, Smokey's rear end wagging like mad as she carried him to the table with Anna and Georgie hot on her heels. I trailed behind, wondering what Barbie might have been thinking, but it would be weeks before I found out just how sneaky my friend could be.

Breakfast and a Breakthrough

As the piles of food disappeared and the conversation around the table ebbed and flowed between topics, my mind returned to August Skies and the three dead bodies. Evelyn was in the brig and would be handed over to the police soon. The murder of Eoin and Scarlet still had to be solved, but I was going to have to leave it for the security team remaining on board to sort out.

Even though I wanted to be the one to crack the case, I had to deal with some of the other issues in my life. This was the first time an investigation had evaded resolution and I was finding it more frustrating than I should.

The news that I was staying on board, or rather, returning to live with Alistair and hopefully taking up a post as the ship's detective was the hottest subject being discussed, but as Rick and Akamu made jokes about the ship suffering because I'm such a trouble-magnet, I saw that Melissa and Paul were keeping quiet.

They were yet to announce a decision about Sam and my suggestion he remain on the Aurelia as my assistant. I understood it wasn't a simple case of letting go – Sam wasn't able to live alone and I would be living with Alistair. That meant a live-in helper for Sam if he were to stay here. Lots of complexities and unknowns for the parents and it wasn't as if he would be in a house a couple of streets away from them; he would be on the other side of the planet.

It probably didn't help that he'd been shot helping me stop a mad man a couple of weeks ago.

I didn't need to press them for an answer now. I couldn't for that matter because Purple Star Cruise Lines were yet to confirm they would create the role of ship's detective and employ me. That Alistair was convinced they would was good enough for me, and I wasn't sure what I might do if they chose not to. However, the Chalks' decision regarding their son could wait … for a while at least.

My silent musings were broken by the sound of my phone ringing. It was attached to a charging lead in the kitchen. I moved to get up but Alistair – sitting next to me - was already rising, collecting dirty crockery and cutlery to clear the table.

'I'll get it, darling,' he announced, making me feel warm inside. It had been a long time since anyone called me darling and meant it.

Alistair snagged the phone and handed it to me screen up so I could see it was Lady Mary calling.

'Mary,' I said in answering it. 'Are you home already?'

'Hello, sweetie,' she replied. 'I'm at Heathrow, actually. I needed to catch up with my husband before he jets off again. I just wanted to wish you a safe trip home.'

'Thank you, Mary. We'll be leaving soon, I think. I'm afraid you missed a wonderful breakfast get together.'

'Yes,' she acknowledged. 'Unfortunate but necessary. I wanted to ask how long you would be home for? Will I get to see you again before you return to the ship?'

'I guess that depends how long you will be away for, Mary.'

'About two weeks,' she told me.

That was going to be cutting it fine. 'I might still be home in two weeks,' I gave her my honest answer. 'But the ship will be in the Mediterranean by then. Our plan was to catch up to it.'

'I see,' she murmured, sounded distracted as if she were thinking of something else. 'Well, look, maybe I'll come to the ship to see you instead.'

'Really?' I laughed. 'Another holiday?'

'No, sweetie. Not a holiday at all. I bumped into August Skies this morning on my way to the helipad. I had no idea he was on board. I've been trying to get him to paint a mural in my house for years, but the man does what he wants when he wants, and no amount of money will change his mind. I'm thinking maybe if I butter him up a bit over a few cheeky cocktails, I can get him to change his mind.'

I blinked a couple of times, my brain replaying her reply. 'You bumped into him?' I tried to confirm.

'Yes, sweetie. Caught him completely off guard. I've never seen a man jump so much as when I called his name.'

My mouth had gone dry. 'What time was this, Mary?'

'Um.' She made me wait while she thought about it. 'I guess ... it must have been about ... threeish. Something like that anyway. Ungodly early, that's what time it was. I didn't exactly want to be out of bed ...' Lady Mary continued to chatter away, saying something about the need to support her husband (international bestselling thriller novelist) and his little hobby.

Her words went into my ears but didn't penetrate the outer layers of my brain because I was too focussed on a singular fact: August Skies hadn't spent the night in bed with his wife at all. He'd been out of bed and wandering the ship at the exact time he would have needed to be if he were to murder Eoin and Scarlet.

I gasped out loud, the sound getting the attention of half the people in the suite and when I grasped the edge of the table to support myself as the world shifted beneath my feet, the rest of them stopped what they were doing to stare my way.

'He used a painting trowel!' I blurted.

'What was that, sweetie?' asked Lady Mary, undoubtedly confused by my outburst.

'Mary, I've got to go. Kisses!' I made a kissy noise as if we were air-kissing goodbye and went to stab the red button to end the call. Just about managing to abort the action before my finger made contact, I put it back to my ear to ask her. 'Can you testify to that?' I begged her.

I got a beat of silence from the other end. 'That I don't have to worry about my husband having affairs because he never looks up from what he is writing?'

Obviously, I'd missed a whole chunk of what she had been telling me. 'No, Mary. That you saw August Skies at around three this morning and he was out of bed?'

'Oh. Well, yes, I guess I could do that. Why?'

'Because I just solved a murder.'

An insistent knock at my door sent the dogs barking and running. Jermaine would deal with it momentarily, not that I could guess who might be outside. I had no time for visitors, that was for sure. I needed to get off the phone so I could call Lieutenant Baker, brush over our fraught discussion earlier and rally him and his colleagues to the Prestwick Suite where we would be making an arrest.

'Mary, I have to go. I'll call you soon.'

I heard her attempt to say goodbye, but I was moving too fast, hanging up the call before she could get the words out.

Everyone in the suite was looking at me – I had their undivided attention. 'August Skies was out of his suite in the night. Lady Mary saw him. He's the killer. He lied about the whole thing. He probably killed Vanessa too. Now that we've caught him in the lie, I bet we can prove the whole thing.' I had an enormous, jubilant smile on my face. It wasn't exactly appropriate but that was how I felt.

From behind me, a voice said, 'I have the proof.' I recognised the voice and knew who it was before I turned around. Lieutenant Baker was standing just inside the main living area of my suite with Jermaine by his side and the familiar forms of Pippin, Bhukari, and Schneider behind him. 'His fingerprints were on the PDA,' he announced, stepping forward with a tablet in his hand.

Were it not an unladylike act, I might have punched the air and cheered.

'That's not all,' claimed another voice. I hadn't seen him because he was standing behind Schneider, unable to get into the suite from the small lobby area because the way was blocked. However, I wasn't the only one who recognised Hideki's voice.

Barbie bounded across the room, her gazelle-like legs bouncing with joy to greet her boyfriend. 'Babes,' she pulled him into a hug as the lieutenants parted to let him through.

Now I was torn because I wanted to hear how August's print came to be found on the PDA when it wasn't there the first time they checked, and I was really keen to hear what Hideki believed to be newsworthy.

I didn't have to choose because Baker spoke first. 'It was on the battery.' He held up the tablet so I could see the picture. It was of the bottom side of Evelyn's PDA where a single small screw held the batteries inside their compartment. 'They hadn't thought to look inside,' he explained.

'How come you did?' asked Alistair, coming closer to see for himself.

Baker's face coloured and his fiancée poked him in the ribs from behind as she chuckled. 'Go on. Tell them.'

I gave Baker a lopsided grin. He and I would talk about our heated discussion later, for now I was enjoying seeing him squirm. 'Yeah, tell us.'

'I saw it on a detective show,' he revealed.

That didn't sound like a reason for embarrassment. I frowned. 'Which one?'

Deepa Bhukari sniggered again.

Lieutenant Baker hung his head. '*Harriet the Spy*.'

A broad smile split my face. The subject of how recently he might have watched the pre-teen television drama needed exploring but now was not the time. The picture of the PDA's battery compartment showed two mismatched batteries, one of which had a distinctive print on it outlined with fingerprinting dust – the technology available to the ship's security team wasn't quite up to modern standards, but they got results, nevertheless.

Hideki stepped in. 'I need to tell you about the first victim.'

'Have you been to bed yet?' I asked, taking in his mussy hair and stubbly chin.

'Not important,' he brushed my question aside. 'There is a burn inside the suicide victim's nostrils. A chemical burn. I didn't see it at first, I guess it's because I wasn't looking for it, but had she been alive, it would have been uncomfortable enough for her to be complaining about it.'

I pictured Vanessa standing on the quayside yesterday afternoon; she seemed excited, which I now knew was probably because she was planning to escape during this trip and was being taken to meet B. When I caught a glimpse of her later inside August's suite, she looked equally untroubled by nasal issues.

'It's fresh,' he said, 'No sign of healing so it would have occurred not long before she died. Not more than a couple of hours.'

My brain came up to speed. 'Paint thinner!' I blurted, thrusting Lieutenant Baker's tablet back into his hands. 'He fed her champagne and oxy, waited for her to drift so she was barely aware of her surroundings, then held a cloth loaded with paint thinners over her nose. There's no bruising because she was out of it already. He wouldn't even need to hold it on hard, just keep it there until she breathed in enough to lose consciousness.' I cursed myself. 'Why didn't I see this before? Somewhere there is a rag loaded with paint thinner and it will have cells from her skin on it as well as his.'

Baker and I were looking right into each other's eyes. Just a couple of hours ago, we'd been standing in front of a man guilty of killing three people and I told him we knew he did it. I took myself back to the stupid poker analogy because what I'd done was not only show him the cards I was holding, I'd told him what cards I would have in my next hand as well.

He knew we were onto him and if he had half a brain, any evidence there was to find had now been destroyed.

A fingerprint on the battery of his ex-wife's PDA showed that he'd touched it, nothing else. It wouldn't get me a conviction. Any lawyer would dismiss it with a few words. The paint thinner burn didn't prove anything either, except perhaps that the poor woman was murdered. What we needed was proper evidence. He lied about being in his bed, but again that wasn't going to put him in jail for life.

Staring at each other, Baker and I reached the same conclusion at the same time. 'We've got to get into his cabin!' we blurted in harmony.

In the next heartbeat, we were running for the door.

On the Run

Schneider and Pippin were still loitering in the lobby of my suite when we started running. Coming right at them, their eyes took on a panicked look before they got the message to their hands and feet. Pippin grabbed the door handle, wrenching it open before we got to it so that a whole column of us funnelled out and into the passageway, turning right at full throttle to run hard for the next suite along.

Puffing along somewhere at the back would be Rick and Akamu, and ahead of me already were the team of security guards, joined swiftly by Barbie as she raced by me in the sudden excitement.

My brain was whirling, giddy with jubilant visions of August Skies in cuffs and of Evelyn finally released. Purple Star Cruise Lines could not help but be impressed and we could all leave the boat and travel home to my little village in Kent with the case neatly sewn up behind us.

Pippin got to the Prestwick Suite door first, where he skidded to a stop and started hammering on the door.

'Just open it!' yelled Lieutenant Baker, running along just ahead of me.

Sam was by my right elbow. 'What's going on, Mrs Fisher?' he asked.

The subtlety of the discovery hadn't been explained in terms he could grasp. He was running because everyone else was running, and before I could answer him, I realised I'd done nothing to contain the dogs.

Three of them whipped by my feet, accelerating hard now they had negotiated the treacherous stampede of feet behind me. I had enough time to shout, 'Dogs, no!' before Pippin swiped his universal card on the suite's door pad. As he shoved the door open, announcing his official presence to the persons inside, three tiny sausage dogs shot through the gap and I got to hear them barking at someone inside.

I yelled for them again, praying they wouldn't bite someone they ought not to – Purple Star would take a dim view to an arrest report where dachshunds were first to tackle the killer.

Schneider barrelled into the Prestwick Suite behind Pippin, closely followed by Bhukari, then Barbie. Baker went through just before me with Sam right on my shoulder and his parents just behind him. Alistair was with me too, and right behind him came Jermaine, Mavis and Agnes, Mike Atwell and last but not least, the two retired Hawaiian cops, Rick and Akamu.

It was quite the team, but as the final pair arrived puffing and panting in the suite's main living area, it was already clear August was gone.

We had been in the suite for no more than five seconds. Long enough to open doors and check the rooms leading off from the central open-plan space. It was also enough time for Barbie, Jermaine and me to scoop the dogs, each of us snagging one as it whizzed by our feet.

I was seething with anger. Not aimed at August so much as at myself. I'd shown him my cards, and August, sensing we would find the missing clue we needed at some point, had chosen to run.

Lieutenants Baker and Bhukari were already on their radios, relaying fast instructions to guards stationed around the ship. The Aurelia was at dock in Southampton. Passengers were getting off and once August was on shore, he could vanish. Who knew what reserves he might have stashed away? On the run, he might be able to use his connections to disappear. I would not find myself shocked to discover he had access to a private island somewhere.

Gerard the butler was standing in the kitchen, neither speaking nor moving, but looking dazed by this development. He was assigned to the suite and his first duty therefore was to the occupants. However, there was a priority above that, and it was to the cruise line, the ship, and his captain.

'Where are they?' demanded Alistair. 'Gerard, where are Mr and Mrs Skies?'

As if shocked by the question, the French butler blurted, 'Mr Skies departed the moment the ship docked, sir. I believe he was heading ashore.'

'Where's Mrs Skies?' I wanted to know. I had questions for her too.

'I am here,' a quiet voice said as Niamh emerged from her bedroom. 'Is he gone?'

Schneider turned his eyes on Pippin, a questioning look because the young man had declared the suite's master bedroom empty.

Pippin's face bore a shocked look of confusion. 'I checked the room and the adjoining bathroom,' he claimed defensively.

'I was hiding in the closet,' Niamh admitted.

'Why?' I frowned, and I was not the only one curious about her desire to hide.

She had a crowd of people staring at her as she stood looking small and frightened in the doorway to her bedroom. Her eyes were cast down at the carpet, unwilling to look at anyone, but she flicked a glance up at me, her cheeks glowing red with embarrassment.

'I'm sorry I lied to you earlier,' she murmured, her voice little more than a whisper. 'He really did it, didn't he?'

Letting a frustrated breath escape my nose, I forced my angry teeth to unclamp so I could say, 'He left the suite in the night, didn't he?'

Her eyes and face were locked on the carpet, but she nodded her head slowly.

Lieutenant Baker grabbed Schneider's arm. 'Get to the dock! Take Pippin and Bhukari. You know his face, get among the crowd and find him!'

There was no discussion or suggestion any of them would challenge his command. They were all the same rank, but Baker was the more senior and recognised by all as the one who took charge. That Alistair was in the room had no bearing on his crew doing their jobs efficiently.

As three white uniforms ran for the door, I focussed my gaze on Niamh. 'Why did you lie?'

She looked up at me now, her face showing no guile or deceit. 'He scares me,' she said, her voice still quiet. 'I don't think he knew I was awake, but he snuck out of bed at two seventeen. I know because I checked the clock. I followed him. I was going to ask him to get me a glass of water – my head was pounding – but I saw him open his toolbox and take out something that glinted in the moonlight coming through the window. I didn't know what it was or what he was doing, but I saw the look on his face when he started toward the door and I froze. I don't know how he didn't see me, but he left, and I went back to bed, too scared to challenge him. When you were here earlier, he came to find me while I was being sick, and he told me I had to say he was in bed with me all night. I knew he would hurt me if I went against him, so I did it; I lied to you.'

My heart pounded in my chest when I saw the toolbox August kept all his artist's equipment in on the deck by the easel. It was closed but I couldn't see a lock on it.

'Stand back,' instructed Lieutenant Baker as he approached it, fishing in his pocket for latex gloves. I don't know about anyone else, but I didn't breathe for the next few seconds while Baker used a tool from his pocket to carefully lift the lid and rummage through the contents.

Nodding his head, he carefully reached in with one gloved hand to remove a small trowel. It was what I'd seen August paint with yesterday.

'Is that blood?' asked Melissa, the horror in her voice apparent for everyone to hear.

'Is it?' asked Alistair, his authority demanding an answer.

Lieutenant Baker locked eyes with his captain and nodded solemnly. 'I believe it is, sir.'

The trowel was perhaps four inches long. Easily long enough to kill a person with. Both the steel of the blade and the wooden handle bore dark stains. Seeing the man in his white uniform begin to struggle taking an evidence bag from his pocket, my assistant, Sam, darted forward.

He'd seen this done many times and knew not to touch anything with his bare hands. I got to see Melissa watch in wonder as her Down Syndrome son carefully slipped on a pair of latex gloves and take the bag to help the security officer. What I knew was going to prove to be the murder weapon went into a bag which Lieutenant Baker then sealed.

'We'll need the whole box,' Baker announced standing up. He didn't make it fully upright before he spotted something and darted back down to get a closer look at it. Motioning to Sam, he produced another evidence bag. Taking it, Sam held it open, peering cautiously into the toolbox to see what Lieutenant Baker had found.

From its depths, Baker extracted what looked to be a glass jam jar. As he turned, I could see it was precisely that and inside it was a rag. My heart skipped because I knew what it was. So did Baker, slowly unscrewing the cap to take a sniff.

'Paint thinner,' he announced. He replaced the lid, but in doing so, he spotted something and held the jar up to the light. 'There is makeup on this rag.'

Lieutenant Bhukari stepped forward, 'Let me see,' she asked, getting in close so she could inspect it. She nodded. 'I think that's Vanessa Morton's shade of lipstick.'

It was all here! All the evidence we could possibly want to find.

With the evidence bags hanging from his left hand, Lieutenant Baker used the right to activate his radio. He was calling in more of the security team, the one who dealt with the forensic element of the work. They had been busy of late and would get no rest any time soon.

Alistair touched my arm. 'I'm heading down to the dock. I know who I'm looking for too.'

'So do I,' I replied, starting toward the suite's door. 'Can we seal off the dock?'

Alistair shook his head. 'Sorry, no. There're too many people involved. I can make the call but doing that will cost other shipping firms millions and cause a blockage with vehicles trying to get in and out. If he gets beyond our quayside area, we may lose him.'

I couldn't let that happen. 'We're coming, Patty,' announced Barbie, hurrying across the suite with Jermaine at her side. They were not alone for it seemed everyone was joining the hunt. They all knew who we were trying to find and were going to willingly lend their eyes to the search.

A second later, we were running again, heading for the nearest elevator.

We left via the royal suites exit at the front of the ship, which is where August had probably gone unless he was paranoid enough to want to use the main exit. If he were running, he probably assumed we were chasing and would have alerted the security guards to look out for him. Coming down in the elevator, Schneider confirmed from the quayside that August had left the ship – the passenger management system had logged him out – but where was he now?

It was possible to walk from the quayside to civilisation, but it was a long way across exposed ground and anyone attempting it would be easy to spot. Most people disembarking now were doing so because this was their home port and they had a car waiting or someone to collect them, or they were here to visit England in which case they would take a taxi, or one of the buses provided.

August, staying in one of the suites would be entitled to use the cruise line's pool of limousines, but a fast conversation with the stewards controlling it confirmed they hadn't seen him.

'Smokey!' the cry of excitement pulled my head around to see where it had come from. Barbie, Jermaine, and I were still holding dachshunds – there just hadn't been time to put them back in our suite. We couldn't put them down either because there were thousands of people on the quayside and the dogs were too dopey to stay with us amid all that excitement.

It had slipped my mind, but Barbie told me Smokey's owner was coming to collect him and that was who called his name. At the barrier rope fifty yards away, an excited woman in her late twenties was frantically waving her right arm while in her left, I could see the flappy ears of a tiny dachshund puppy.

Tucked under my left arm, Smokey barked and wiggled, frantically trying to free himself because he'd seen a human he knew. Spinning around as I was, trying to spot August and then getting distracted by Smokey's owner, his sudden desire to be free caught me unprepared.

He popped free of my arm, but he was three feet off the ground which made me lunge to catch him again. For anyone watching, it must have looked like a strange new circus act where the woman juggled the sausage dog. He kept trying to run even as I was trying to get him safely to the tarmac.

Once close enough that he wouldn't break his stumpy legs, I let him go and watched as he took off like a scalded cat.

Around me, the team were fanning out, merging with the crowd as they tried to find our killer. It truly felt like a race against time to find him at one of the taxi queues or schooched down out of view on one of the buses getting ready to leave the port. I wanted to find him more than I wanted to do anything else, but I had to follow Smokey and at least explain myself.

Jogging to her, which had to look out of place, I waved and started speaking almost before I was within earshot. 'Hi, I'm Patricia. You must be Sarah.'

Sarah had Smokey in her arms, the puppy plopped on the ground and all but forgotten as she hugged and kissed her dog. That she was Smokey's owner could be in no doubt for he was licking her face and whining with excitement at their reunion.

It was lovely to see but at the same time it made me sad because I knew I would be saying goodbye to a dog who'd found a place in my heart.

Tears streamed down Sarah's face, but she was smiling and happy. 'Oh, my gosh. I never thought I would see you again, you silly dog. Where did you get to, eh? You've been on quite the adventure, haven't you,' she gushed as he continued to lick her face and nibble at her ears.

I was forced to wait, resigning myself to do so politely, and trusting the rest of the team to find August Skies while I was distracted. When Sarah Flett looked my way, I offered her a smile and said, 'His things are still in my suite. I'll have to go back for them.' She looked confused, probably questioning why on Earth I would come down to hand him over and not bring his things. To explain, I said, 'You saw the group I came out with? We're on the lookout for someone. A person suspected of a crime and there wasn't time to waste.'

Her eyebrows lifted in response; it wasn't the kind of explanation one hears every day. What she said was, 'Not many people have come out of that exit and I've been standing here since before the first passengers started getting off.'

'That sounds about right,' I sighed. 'He probably went out of the main exit to avoid us.'

'Oh, well, what did he look like?' Sarah asked.

I doubted she was going to be of any help, but looking around now, I couldn't see a single one of my friends. They had all scattered, roaming the crowd and probably boarding busses as they tried to foil August's escape.

With another frustrated sigh, I said, 'Sixties, tall and thin, with a shock of unkempt, wavy grey hair pulled into a loose ponytail.' It was a good enough description. She would either have seen him or she would not have. I suspected the former and was unprepared for her reply.

'You mean August Skies?' she asked innocently. 'The famous artist?'

I lunged forward, grabbing her by the shoulders. 'Which way did he go?' My sudden invasion of her personal space and demand for information caused her to flinch and reel backward, but my grip held her in place. 'Which way, Sarah!' I yelled, thinking I might shake her if she didn't start talking.

She shook herself free, frowning at me like I had gone mad, but she shifted Smokey so he was under her left arm then pointed with her right. 'He's over there.'

I tracked her arm, squinting along the quayside to find a lone figure standing four or five hundred yards beyond the prow of the ship. Even at this distance, I could tell it was him.

Forgetting Sarah Flett in an instant, my feet began to drag me in August Skies' direction. He wasn't trying to get away, so what was he doing? I was too far away to see detail; it was his grey ponytail flapping in the breeze that gave him away, but he appeared to be standing stock still as if frozen to the spot.

I looked around again, trying to find one of my friends. I didn't have a radio. I didn't have my phone. My handbag was still on the counter in my suite where I'd left it. Behind me as I walked toward the front of the ship, the mass of passengers getting off continued to move toward the available transport. My team were in there somewhere, common sense dictating I find at least one of them before I approach a man guilty of three murders.

I wanted to. I really did. But I wasn't going to run the risk of him escaping. If I went for help, would he still be there when I looked again? What was he doing so far away from everyone else anyway? Accepting that there was no time to do anything other than trust to luck, I set off to get him.

Yeah. Patricia Fisher, five foot something middle-aged woman with no fighting ability. I was the perfect choice to wrestle a murderer into submission and drag him to justice.

My nervousness grew with every step. This was a bad thing because there were lots of steps between where I started out and where August Skies still lingered. Having questioned why he was so far from the ship, I figured it was most likely so someone could pick him up without getting caught in all the traffic congregating where all the other passengers were.

He had something in his hands, which when I first spotted it, made my heart rate spike. However, as I drew nearer, I saw it was a camera. The crazed killer was taking snap shots of the ship. Was this a form of trophy taking? I'd heard and read about serial killers keeping mementos of their kills; a token by which they could remember and celebrate the murder.

It was macabre and not for the first time, my brain attempted to convince my feet to turn around to walk the other way. I was out beyond the prow of the ship now, halfway between it and the killer artist. It wasn't too late to turn back, but I knew I wasn't going to. Would he have a weapon about his person? It was a worrying question that had only just occurred to me.

I let my feet stray toward the edge of the dock so I could look over the edge to the water below. It was thirty or more feet to the surface, but if he came at me with a knife, I would run and jump without hesitation.

What if he doesn't pull a knife, Patricia? The unwelcome question bounced around in my head as I tried to work out how I might attempt to subdue him. I felt certain someone would see a fight taking place, but against a man who was taller and stronger than me, how badly would I fair? A terrified chuckle escaped my lips as I considered the hero points I might gain by choosing to battle a killer toe to toe myself. I was going to end up with split lips, black eyes, a nose which would require surgery to straighten, and August might still escape before anyone could get to us.

Perhaps facial injuries would be of help at the divorce meeting, I joked darkly though there was nothing funny about my current situation.

Now that I had walked another hundred yards, August's indistinct outline was taking shape and I could see that he had spotted me. He didn't bolt though, which made me question why for a second. Only for a second though because I realised that he could see all the way back to the ship and knew I was alone.

I didn't turn around to check because I already felt exposed enough without seeing just how far from safety I'd chosen to stray.

August raised the camera to take a few more pictures and I was close enough now to hear the camera working. He clicked off a dozen shots before lowering the camera and looking my way. He was waiting for me to arrive but now that I was close enough to see his features, his expression showed me nothing but mild curiosity.

'Mrs Fisher,' he called when I got to thirty yards away. 'Have you come to see the sunlight? One has to catch it just right. That's the secret so many fail to learn. As it continues to rise, so the position relative to the subject ...'

I cut him off. 'We found the murder weapon, August.'

He fell silent, absorbing the news for a second while he looked confused at my interruption. 'Oh. Well, that's good then,' he replied, lifting the camera once more.

'We found your print on Evelyn's PDA too.'

He clicked a few shots and I wondered if he simply hadn't heard me or was stalling while he decided what to do. I'd come to a stop five yards from him; close enough for conversation, and far enough away to give me reaction time if I needed it.

I was about to speak again when he lowered the camera and fixed with me with a questioning look. 'Evelyn's PDA?'

'Yes, August. You were not as careful as you thought. I have you bang to rights.'

His eyebrows shifted about as if trying to make sense of what I was telling him. 'I'm sorry,' he stuttered. 'I'm not following. What are you trying to tell me?'

'You killed Vanessa when you found out she was using this trip to meet a person she'd found via the internet. She was going to escape you and you could not handle the rejection. You put a fake note on Evelyn's PDA that would point to her, undoubtedly rejoicing when we found it and took the bait. Then you killed Scarlet because she was sleeping with Eoin. I'm guessing you didn't previously know about the second betrayal and their deaths were a knee-jerk reaction. Did Vanessa tell you in her last moments?'

His face was no longer showing me the questioning look of confusion. In its place was an angry mask, a twisted look of hate as he glared at me.

'I already told you I had nothing to do with Vanessa's death,' he growled. 'I certainly didn't kill Scarlet and Eoin. How could I? Niamh already told you I was in bed with her all night.'

He hadn't rushed me yet. I still felt massively exposed, but the longer I could keep him talking, the more likely it was someone would spot me and come to my rescue before he tried to kill me.

'Niamh lied earlier though, didn't she, August? You didn't stay in bed all night at all.' He tilted his head, daring me to prove he was lying. 'Do you know Lady Mary Bostihill-Swank?'

His eyes became unfocussed as he tried to recall from where he knew the name. I saw him mouth the words.

'She has been pestering you to paint a mural in her house. According to her, she has offered you ridiculous sums of money, yet you keep saying no. She doesn't know of your hatred for monetary worth.' I saw the dots connect as his expression changed. 'Perhaps you've never met her so don't know her face, but she was on board last night. She saw you moving about the ship on her way to board her helicopter.'

His cheeks flushed as the inescapable truth of his lie was exposed. 'So what?' he snapped. 'Niamh asked me to find her some painkillers. She woke with a splitting headache from drinking such a stupid amount of whisky. She wanted something stronger than we had in the cabin, so I went to find a medical station.'

A convenient excuse but not one that explained his need to lie. 'Why didn't you just call room service? Why not wake your butler, Gerard, and send him for them?'

'Why have feet at all?' he shot back. 'Everyone is so lazy these days. It's a wonder obesity isn't a bigger problem.'

If we checked, would we find that he had indeed gone to a medical station to obtain some painkillers? I would not be surprised if he'd opted to devise a reason for being out of bed, yet he'd lied about it, only admitting the truth now.

'Why did you lie about it earlier?' I wanted to know.

He sneered at me and lifted his camera to take more pictures. 'Because I recognise what you are, Mrs Fisher – a busybody. You'll stick your nose where it isn't wanted and keep picking away at me even though I have done nothing wrong. I could tell yesterday that you had already decided I was guilty. I think you were yet to decide what I was guilty of, but I was guilty, nevertheless. Now you have some rubbish piece of evidence you are trying to link back to me in the vain hope of what? Framing me for three murders?'

A choke of laughter escaped my lips. 'Framing you?' I repeated. 'I have all the evidence I will need to have you convicted, August Skies. You killed three people in a day and there is no chance that you will get away with it.'

The camera fell from his hands to be caught by the strap around his neck. Behind where it had been, his face was a thunderous boiling sea of rage. A cry of anger escaped his lips, and he came for me.

I'd been pushing him, hoping I could get him to admit something that would seal the conviction, but my goading had gone too far, and he was going to try to silence me instead.

With a squeal of fright, I jerked away from him, backing up and trying to turn at the same time. My feet twisted on themselves, tripping me as I attempted to make them move faster than they were able to go. I went down, thrusting out my arms so I wouldn't fall all the way to the ground and carried on pumping with my legs.

'You awful woman!' August roared. 'Why can't you leave me alone to paint? That's all I want!'

I skinned both my hands, tearing holes in my palms as I scrambled for purchase. Thrusting upward with both arms, I must have looked like a sprinter coming out of a set of blocks. My torso was parallel to the ground and my arms and legs were driving me forward. I was a decade younger than the artist; maybe I could outrun him.

I got my answer half a second later when he slammed into me from behind.

I guess not then.

The air whooshed from my lungs as I hit the unforgiving tarmac of the dock and pain reported in from dozens of body parts simultaneously.

'I have important work to do!' August screamed from behind my head. 'Why must people interfere?'

It was a good question and one which I was currently asking myself. Though saying that now, at the time I had been unable to form rational thoughts because I was terrified for my life and scared he might be about to stab me with a knife or just throttle the life right out of me.

When his weight suddenly vanished from my back in the next instant, I had no idea why until I heard Barbie's voice.

'Patty! Are you okay?' she gasped.

I didn't get to answer because Georgie climbed my face, licking my front teeth before I could get my mouth shut and robbing me of a breath I desperately needed to take.

August slammed face first into the dock next to me, an arm bent cruelly behind his back as Jermaine ensured he could do nothing else to harm me.

I rolled onto my back and let Barbie help me into a sitting position. More people were arriving – the whole team, I saw. They were piling out of limousines which they'd used to close the distance from the ship to where they spotted me with August.

Alistair threw himself down next to me, taking hold of my hand gently. Looking into my eyes, he said, 'Patricia, you have a habit of making my days more adventurous than I might otherwise like.'

As Pippin and Bhukari took over from Jermaine, hauling August to his feet to take him away, I offered Alistair a tired smile. 'Welcome to England.'

Return of a Friend

I elected to walk back along the quayside rather than take the offered limousine. It wasn't that I needed the exercise, but because Alistair was holding my hand and I didn't want to let it go. The palms of my hands were bleeding in several places where gravel on the ground had torn through the soft flesh. So too my elbows and knees and my outfit was good for the trash now with rips and scuffs in multiple places.

Over the next two hours, Jermaine and a team of stewards packed up the rest of my belongings and transferred it down to the quayside. My minor wounds were tended and dressed in my suite while I drank tea and petted Anna and Georgie. I couldn't tell if they were aware of Smokey's absence and affected by it or whether they would miss him. He was gone when we got back to the royal suite's entrance. Sarah, his owner, most likely confused by what she had seen, chose not to wait for the rest of Smokey's things. I probably wouldn't have either.

I would get her number from Barbie and call to explain it all once we were home. For now, I was content that she had been reunited with her dog and had gone out to get a puppy in the time that he was missing. Like me she now had two funny little sausage dogs and they would entertain and provide company for each other much as mine did.

Alistair was ready to go, his replacement up to speed and probably eager to get him off the ship so she could relax. He was to meet me shortly once his luggage was ready. Melissa and Paul came by my suite on their way out.

'Are you off?' I asked them.

Melissa said, 'We're just going now, Patricia.' Sam was loitering behind, hanging around at the door for some reason. I found out why when Melissa added, 'About Sam joining you and staying here on the ship,' she started. I kept quiet so she could find the words she wanted. 'I don't want him to stay here.' I accepted the news silently. It was disappointing but I had half expected it. 'But,' Melissa continued, 'I don't feel that it would be fair for us to stop him when he is clearly doing something he loves.' In the space of a second my heart went from gloomy to thrilled.

Paul added, 'We saw him earlier, assisting Lieutenant Baker. I've never seen Sam look so focussed and involved.'

Melissa had a catch in her throat when she said, 'It will be a tough adjustment, but if it is what he wants, then we will not stand in his way.'

I met them both with my most reassuring smile. 'I promise to do my best to protect him and keep him safe. I haven't worked out all the details,' I admitted. 'Like who will look after his needs on a daily basis, but I expect to be able to hire someone.' Someone like Molly my former housemaid was what I had in mind. If she hadn't already left my employment to train as a security guard for Purple Star, then I would be suggesting the job to her.

Melissa said, 'We'll see you back home, I expect. You can let us know when you plan to return to the ship.'

'We'll have Sam ready,' added Paul.

They started to back away, heading for the door to collect Sam. There was a limousine waiting to take them home courtesy of Alistair making arrangements through Purple Star. I knew they had been excited about getting away on holiday and had viewed the cruise as a once in a lifetime opportunity. Now that it was done, I couldn't be sure how they would remember it, but it is always nice to get home and Sam was keen to get back to his puppy who'd been left with a neighbour for their trip.

Just after the Chalks left, Lieutenant Baker knocked on my door. As was commonplace, he had Lieutenant Schneider with him. The security guards almost always travelled in pairs and I saw these two together more often than not. If Baker wasn't with Schneider, then it would be Bhukari, his intended.

'The local police are here to take August Skies away,' Baker announced, settling into a couch opposite me. 'How are you feeling?' He was asking about my cuts and bruises, I thought. Not my state of mind over leaving the Windsor Suite.

'My injuries are minor,' I replied, finishing my tea, and setting the cup and saucer to one side. 'What will happen to August now?'

Baker removed the electronic tablet from the side pocket on his trousers. 'That's why we are here, actually, Mrs Fisher. We need a statement from you before you leave. The local police will hold him until he can be transferred. Because he is an Irish national who perpetrated crimes only on other Irish nationals, the matter is far less complicated than normal. He will be handed over to the Garda who will treat and try him as if the crimes had occurred on Irish soil.'

I nodded along as he spoke. Dealing with crime at sea always brought a headache because the nationalities of the criminal and the victim were rarely the same. Then one had to take into consideration whether they were in international waters at the time of the crime, or in an area designated to a given country. The country under which the ship was registered also played a part. Let's just say they were right to be glad this one appeared to be simple.

'How long will that take?' I asked.

'To hand him over to the Garda?' Lieutenant Baker sought to confirm. 'Not long. A day, at least, though. They'll fly someone in from Ireland to get him and fly him back.'

His answers satisfied my curiosity. 'Where do you want to record my statement? Do you have an interview room in mind?' I just wanted to get it done so we could all get going. Daylight was wasting and though it was barely noon, I wanted to get home and unpacked in time to see the village with Alistair.

Baker fiddled with his tablet, setting it on the coffee table between us as he said, 'I think we can just do it here, Mrs Fisher.'

This wasn't my first statement to the Aurelia's security team. In fact, I had to wonder if any passenger had ever given more than me. It was finished in under fifteen minutes, the two lieutenants guiding me through my account of the events with a focus on our exchange at the quayside.

Just as we finished up, Barbie came out of her bedroom carrying two sports bags over her shoulders. 'That's the last of it,' she announced, dropping them both to the carpet. She spotted the lieutenants. 'Oh, hey, guys.'

They both dipped their heads to thank me for my time and got to their feet. 'Hey, Barbie,' said Lieutenant Baker. 'All set?'

She frowned, her lips pursed to display that she wasn't entirely happy. 'I just got Hideki here to be with me and now I'm leaving again. I feel like we are passing ships.' Sensing that she was beginning to whine, she chuckled at herself. 'Listen to me with my first world problems. It's only for a week or maybe two, right Patty?'

I thought about her question. 'I need to stay until my divorce is finalised, but you and Jermaine could hot foot it back to the ship and meet it at the next port in a couple of days. You're only coming with me so you can get the rest of your belongings.'

'That's true,' she admitted. 'Though you know Jermaine will never willingly leave your side, so if I do come back, I'll be doing it by myself.'

'We really have to get going,' announced Lieutenant Baker, turning toward the door as he pocketed his tablet once more. 'We look forward to seeing you all soon. I hope you can get back for the wedding.'

My jaw dropped open. 'I'd totally forgotten about that! When is it?'

Baker reminded me of the date. It was the following Saturday! He and Deepa Bhukari were set to be wed on the open upper deck of the Aurelia with the captain leading the ceremony. They had a few family members flying in to attend as the ship was due to be docked in Naples on its way around the Mediterranean Sea. The rest of the attendees would be friends on board. Would I be back? I would hate to miss it and I knew Barbie would too.

Grimacing, I said, 'I'll do my best, but I have no control over events that might keep me in England.'

Baker nodded his understanding and withdrew, repeating his wish for us to have a good trip as both men went out the door. My shout made them pop their heads back around the door frame, Schneider, the tall Austrian's above Baker's but nothing else showing as if it were just two heads.

'Mrs Fisher?' Baker questioned.

'Evelyn Skies. Did you release her?'

Lieutenant Baker backtracked a pace so he was visible again. 'I have ordered her release. She may already be out, but if not, she will be soon. I will of course check on her and having delivered the news about August, will need to take another statement.'

Something made the back of my skull itch. I tried to focus on what I might have missed. Was there something in my statement that was wrong? Or had I failed to include something which might prove pivotal at his trial?

So focussed on revisiting all that had happened since leaving Dublin, I didn't hear Lieutenant Baker trying to get my attention until Barbie tapped my arm. I looked up.

'We really have to go, Mrs Fisher. Have a good trip.'

There was no chance to reply because he was gone, the sound of his feet running down the passageway outside telling me he'd already stayed too long.

The moment they were gone, Barbie asked, 'Will you miss this place?' She was looking around the suite longingly. 'I know I will. Hideki's quarters are nice. Much nicer than the regular crew get since he's a doctor and all. But it's not like this.'

I looked about, taking it all in and committing as much of it as possible to memory just like I had the last time I left. The Windsor Suite was something else. The lap of luxury on the top deck of the world's most luxurious cruise liner. How could I ever top it? Even my seventy-three-bedroom manor house back in Kent couldn't meet the mark. Largely that was because my home in Kent didn't sail around the world while I slept, delivering me to a fantastic and exotic new location each morning.

It was something from a child's fantasy book but somehow there was no magic involved. After a few seconds, I tore my eyes away. Knowing I would never see it again, I could treasure the memories, but there was nothing to be gained by torturing myself.

To answer my blonde friend's question, I said. 'Yes, I will miss it. I will be with Alistair though and that is compensation enough.'

He arrived less than a minute later, knocking on the doorframe, and fixing me with a smile. 'Are you ready, my lady?'

Jermaine appeared behind him. 'All your luggage is loaded, madam.' He had secured a small van to take it all back to my house; there was just too much to fit into one of the cruise line's limousines. Having flown out of the country to meet the ship in Canada, all our cars were still at the house, so it was to be a limousine that took us home. It wasn't exactly a hardship and though I hadn't voiced it, my plan was to snuggle up next to Alistair and fall asleep on the ninety-minute drive – Lord knows I needed to catch up on some missed shut eye. I just hoped I wouldn't dribble on him.

Nodding my head as I took one last look around, I collected the two dog leads and my handbag, checked down the back of the sofa for some unaccountable reason and took Alistair's arm when he offered it.

I will admit I felt a little odd leaving the suite this time. More so than the first time I departed the ship after my three-month trip around the world. However, any sense of ill-feeling I might have felt faded away the moment I walked down the gangplank and saw an old friend waiting for me.

'Oh, no you didn't!' I squealed.

Parked at the pickup point where the next passengers in line would expect to find one of the sleek black cruise line limousines was an Aston

Martin DB2/4 Drophead Coupé. Or, to be more accurate, it was my Aston Martin DB2/4 Drophead Coupé.

The last time I saw it, the poor wreck of a car was being towed away by a specialist repair firm who promised to do their best to restore it to its former glory. Well, they had outdone themselves – it looked brand new.

A pair of the Godmother's assassins had shot it into pieces, leaving it looking like Swiss cheese. The exterior bodywork, the wonderful walnut dashboard, the sumptuous leather upholstery – all had been destroyed, but rushing forward to inspect it, I could see it had been returned to factory line perfection.

It was too pristine for me to touch. I spun around to pin Jermaine to the spot with a look of disbelief. 'You never said it was fixed. Why didn't you say it was being delivered here?'

With an innocent face, he said, 'What would be the fun in that, madam?'

'That's quite the car,' commented Rick, ambling across the quayside toward me, Akamu and the girls on his tail and Mike Atwell bringing up the rear.

I turned to speak to him, but my reply got caught in my mouth because Barbie had moved to intercept. She was standing between me and the party from Zangrabar. She had something to say and she was saying it quietly, her head right up against Rick's so she could whisper in his ear. Akamu was listening in too, both men nodding when she finished whatever it was she had to say. When she stepped away, Rick was holding an envelope he hadn't been a moment before.

I squinted at it, only to have him whip it away behind his back. 'That's quite the car,' Rick repeated his previous sentence. He was up to something. Or, rather, Barbie was up to something and Rick was participating.

I narrowed my eyes at him, but said, 'It's my Aston Martin.'

Akamu gave a low whistle of appreciation. 'You don't get much more British than that, Brah.'

Mavis cleared her throat audibly and tapped her watch when the chaps looked her way.

'Our flight is in two hours,' Agnes reminded them.

I stepped forward and threw an arm around Rick's neck, motioning for Akamu to come close enough that I could hug him too.

'I'm going to miss you, guys,' I all but sobbed. 'You saved my life this time. Thanks for coming to rescue me.' Would I have survived the Godmother without them? There was no way of knowing but the answer was probably not and that they answered the call and came to my help was enough to make me eternally grateful.

I let them go; they really did need to hustle, or they would miss their flight and they still needed to sneak Mavis and Agnes - two internationally renowned con artists and thieves – through security and passport control. I knew they had fake passports, but the task would make me nervous.

Backing away, Akamu said, 'If you're ever in Zangrabar ...'

I had so many things I wanted to say, but I let them go with a sad wave as a solitary tear ran down my cheek. As the car with my friends from Zangrabar departed, I was left looking at Mike Atwell, the police detective sergeant from my home town. 'Are you heading straight back to Kent?' I asked him. Like the others, he had dropped what he was doing and took time off to help me with the Godmother.

'I have a sister living not far from here. Her husband retired recently. I'm going to spend the night with them and travel home tomorrow. Try not to uncover any diabolical crimes in the village before I get there, please.' He laughed at me, thinking himself quite the card.

'Don't worry, Mike,' I replied. 'I'll be sure to wait until you are around. It's not as much fun if it's only my life on the line.'

We hugged quickly and when we broke apart, he collected two suitcases and started back toward the press of passengers and the car park from where he was probably to be collected.

Watching him go, and about to go home, I thought to myself that everything was so perfect.

So why did I feel like something was wrong?

Unable to articulate what was bothering me, I pushed the concerned thoughts from my head and slid into my car. I had been looking forward to dozing in the back of a limousine, but this was an entirely different proposition. The Aston was thrilling to drive and getting back inside it made me excited about being back home in England.

The van with our luggage was waiting for us, so once everyone was in – the car could take four (just about) – I slid the gearstick into first and aimed the car for home.

Old Enemy

Alistair Huntley, the captain of a cruise ship, is about as well travelled as a person can get. Not only has he been around the world many, many times and explored more countries than most people can name, he was born to an Italian American mother and South African Belgian father. Raised while travelling because his parents were in the cruise line business too, he wasn't really from anywhere.

The very first day I met him, I found his accent hard to place and only found out a month later - when I plucked up the courage to ask him - why that was.

Despite all the travelling, he'd never been to my part of the world and spent the whole trip staring out of the window at the scenery going by. I took him the scenic route along the A25, avoiding the motorway and adding at least an hour to our trip as I slowly wound through ancient village after ancient village. Wide village greens now designated for playing cricket on appeared to our left and right, each of them sporting at least one ancient country pub.

We chatted about the village I grew up in, something we had discussed before but never in any detail and about the investigation business I was going to have to now abandon.

Along the way, I began to feel a sense of ... something. I couldn't put my finger on it and kept finding myself distracted by the conversation in the car. There was something about August and the three murders that wasn't quite right. Like I'd forgotten to tell anyone about a big piece of evidence I had seen. Not that it would make much difference, I didn't think. There was enough evidence to tie him to the crimes and he would crack under police interrogation once they got him back to Ireland.

The A25 weaves through the south east of England, going up and down over the undulating hills and we stayed on it until it brought us to East Malling, my birthplace and home.

'This is it?' asked Alistair, looking through the front screen. In full autumn, the trees were all bare, so too most of the hedgerows but the lack of green did little to diminish the beauty of the place. We passed the church where I was theoretically still a member of the council.

Thinking of the church council, a smile creased my face when an image of Angelica Howard-Box, the council president, appeared. She loathed me and must have loved my sudden absence.

Seeing that Alistair was looking at me curiously, I chose to explain, giving him all the juicy details on my arch nemesis and her campaign of hate against me. Jermaine added details here and there and Barbie tried to tell Alistair about the poster campaign but had to keep stopping because she was laughing so hard.

'And you did what to deserve such focussed attention?' Alistair wanted to know.

'Stole her boyfriend,' I admitted.

My answer surprised him. 'Recently?' he enquired.

I laughed at him, unable to contain my grin. 'We were eight.'

Now he laughed too.

I rounded the next corner, and the post office came into view. 'Have we provisions at the house?' I asked Jermaine, flicking my eyes up to look at him in the rear-view mirror.

'Not yet, madam. With the cook in jail and the house maid employed elsewhere, it was not possible to make suitable arrangements.' He was making excuses though there was no need; he already looked after my every need.

With a flick of the indicator, I slowed the car and pulled into the post office car park. 'I need a cup of tea,' I explained. 'And for that we need milk, so we might as well pull together a basket of provisions to keep us going for a few hours. We can eat out tonight and get a proper shopping trip done tomorrow.'

Knowing Jermaine, he would wait until I was asleep tonight and then fill the larder and refrigerator with all the goods I might want. He was sneaky like that.

Everyone clambered out, taking the opportunity to stretch their legs even though this would be a short stop and we would be home soon. Anna and Georgie, who were asleep on the back seats with Barbie and Jermaine, came awake the instant the car stopped and were bouncing on their back legs in their desperation to get out.

That their excitement might be driven by the possibility of squirrels to chase - something you don't get many of on a cruise ship – wasn't lost on me and I made sure they were being held tight before I opened the door.

Jermaine offered to walk them while the rest of us went into the village store to grab a few essentials. It is a truth of many villages across the nation that the post office, which often doubles as the local store, is the hub of all gossip and activity. You might think it would be the public house, if a village has one, but that is rarely, if ever, true. Some gossiping takes place at church, of course. Good people professing their Christian charity while nudging the person next to them and spreading a rumour that may or may not be true but is too interesting and juicy to keep quiet about.

However, the post office is where it is at, and in the case of East Malling, that is all to do with the lady behind the post office counter.

A bell above the door jingled politely as I went inside. Sharon, the sullen teenager manning the till, lifted her eyes from a trashy magazine just long enough to see who it was before letting them drop back to the article she had been reading.

A sudden gasp of air caught my attention, pulling my eyes around to find someone I didn't want to see glaring at me. 'What are you doing here?' sneered Angelica Howard-Box in the same tone one might reserve for stepping in something unpleasant.

Carefully, and minding my manners, I said, 'I live here. Remember?'

Angelica was shaking her head as if witness to a sudden and terrible sight that she could see but refused to believe. 'No,' she stammered. 'No, no, no. You left. Poof, you were gone, and it was like all my dreams had come true.'

A cackling noise coming from behind Angelica turned out to be Mavis. There was a queue for the post office counter but she'd abandoned them so she could get a closer look at the two of us facing off.

'Who is this?' Alistair whispered from the corner of his mouth. Staying to one side and not getting involved, he nevertheless found himself fascinated.

'The sour faced old cow is Angelica,' Barbie replied, speaking for me, and doing nothing to lower her voice. Angelica didn't flinch at the bold insult, her eyes locked on mine and a grimace on her face.

I added, 'The lady behind her is Mavis. She's the post office clerk.'

Mavis continued to laugh, and it was all aimed at Angelica. 'I told you she wasn't dead, Angelica.' Sensing that some explanation was required, Mavis added, 'You were just gone one morning, Patricia. Your house was shut up and the post was all being redirected here. I've got a big pile of it in the back. Angelica started a rumour that you were dead because you were either a criminal, and had fallen foul of your own misdoings. Or … what was your other theory, Angelica?'

Angelica had the decency to blush. 'I have never started a rumour in my life,' she lied. 'I merely suggested that after the shoot out on the bypass and the one which destroyed my house, the people after you had probably succeeded.'

Mavis clicked her fingers, remembering the thing that had eluded her. 'Devil worship. That was it. Angelica suggested you were involved in satanic practices and had been dragged to hell where you belong.'

'Well, I'm afraid your place on the church council has been filled already,' Angelica sneered. 'There'll be a long wait before you can reapply.'

'Or I could just speak to the vicar,' I suggested. 'He always liked my can-do attitude.'

Angelica sucked in a breath to start arguing, probably about to point out that she ran the church council, but I held up a hand to stop her before she could get started.

'Don't worry, Angelica, I'm not staying. I have some personal business to attend to and then I will be on my way again. I'll be back one day, but you should be safe from the evil you're convinced I encourage for a while.'

I reached out with my left hand to hook Alistair's elbow. I was done talking to the village's one truly nasty piece of work, but she had a final question.

'How soon will you be going?' she wanted to know.

I almost answered, but the hopeful tone of her voice made me stop. I looked at her, assessing the woman who would happily see me in a coffin. 'Why?'

Maybe Angelica would have answered honestly and maybe she wouldn't. She didn't get the chance to do either because Mavis said, 'It's her son's wedding next weekend.'

Angelica's cheeks coloured again.

I shot her a wolfish grin. 'I had no idea. I expect my invitation is in that pile of mail Mavis has for me.'

Angelica spluttered her horror. 'You're not to come within a hundred yards of the venue, Patricia Fisher! I'll not have you turn Kent's wedding of the year into an utter farce.' Her indignant outrage was just fuel for me.

'Where is it?' I asked, and again it was Mavis who provided the answer.

'Loxton Hall.'

Angelica shot the post office clerk a hateful look and got a grin in return. Then her eyes swung back to me and she stepped into my personal space. 'I have hired the best venue in the county. I have Felicity Phillips, the county's best wedding planner at the helm and no less than four magazines running articles on the event. If I see you anywhere near Loxton Hall next weekend … if I even hear a rumour that you have driven by, I will shoot you, Patricia Fisher. I will take my shotgun and I will end your menace to this community once and for all.'

I grinned in her face. Truth is, she probably meant it. She was just about crazy enough to think she could justify killing me for the good of the village and possibly the world.

Alistair stepped between us, looking down at my enemy with his gorgeous eyes. 'I think perhaps you ought to move along, madam,' he said, his voice like steel.

Angelica stepped away and put one hand on the door to leave. 'Go back to that ship of yours, Patricia. Go back and never return.' Just in case I might have a final word of my own lined up, she shoved the door and left before it could be delivered. The little bell jingled again, the only sound in the otherwise deathly silent shop.

'She doesn't like me,' I explained to Alistair flippantly.

He picked up a basket so we could begin to load groceries and said, 'No. I very much get that impression.' He was silent for a beat, his face showing that he had something else he wanted to say. 'You know, I can't help feeling that I would like to stay here until at least after next weekend. Tell me, is Loxton Hall nice?'

By the Light of the Moon

Rather than go out to eat, Alistair found in the local store all he needed to cook what he claimed to be his personal speciality go-to Italian meatball dish. Paired with a decent bottle of red wine, which I knew we could take from the cellar at my house, we had an evening of each other's company planned.

Alistair marvelled at the house the same way everyone does. That was before we got inside it and he saw just how opulent my surroundings were. Barbie giggled at him, making a comment about the car collection which of course prompted a visit to the garage.

Seeing the array of fantastic cars, his eyes lit up like a child in a toyshop.

The rest of the afternoon and evening passed in a blur. Jermaine and Barbie made their excuses, leaving the house to go out for food instead which I believe was a subtle way of leaving Alistair and me to have dinner by the open fire in the kitchen.

I was happy, relaxed, and content. There was kissing and more, but behind it all, I still couldn't shift the feeling that I had forgotten to mention something in my statement about August. Was that it? I kept going around in a circle, unable to shift the worrying feeling that I had forgotten something or missed something, but unable to pin down what it might be.

While Alistair slept soundly next to me in my giant bed in my giant bedroom, I stared at the ceiling and slowly drove myself mad.

That went on for two hours while the moon slowly shifted across the sky outside my window. I kept shutting my eyes and trying to think of boring things to help me sleep. Nothing seemed to work, and restless, I got up to close the curtains.

Perhaps making the room darker would help me to find sleep.

Gripping the curtains of one window, I stopped moving, my jaw hanging slackly as the thing I had missed bobbed to the surface.

The moon.

What about it, Patricia? Someone had said something about the moon, and it didn't fit. That was what had been bothering me. Now I just had to force my sleep-deprived brain to remember who said what.

It was ... I couldn't see it. The memory refused to coalesce, so I knew it was there, hiding just out of sight, but couldn't see it no matter what I tried.

The hand on my waist made me scream. Somewhere inside my head I knew it was Alistair touching me, but he'd been in bed and I hadn't heard him move.

When my ear-splitting shriek subsided, he asked, 'Are you all right, Patricia?'

It was a good thing my bladder was empty before I went to bed. 'Yes,' I managed to blurt as I fell against the window and used it to keep myself upright. 'Wow, that made me jump.'

The sound of running feet outside preceded a hasty, insistent knocking on my bedroom door. 'Are you all right, madam?' asked Jermaine through the closed door.

I called back, 'Yes, Jermaine. Something startled me. That's all.' But it wasn't all because the shock made my brain skip forward and now I could hear the lie in my head.

Why Lie?

Knowing there was no way I could sleep now and that I needed to make some phone calls, I threw on a dressing gown and slippers to head downstairs.

'Niamh lied,' I told the three people following me down the house's sweeping staircase. My behaviour required some explanation and yet again, I was denying them sleep when it was probably the one thing in the world they craved more than anything else.

'Lied about what?' Alistair wanted to know.

Back in the kitchen, with my phone poised in my right hand, I filled in a few blanks. 'Niamh stated that she saw August leaving the suite with one of his painting trowels in his hand. She could see him because the moon was shining brightly through the window.' My finger was hovering over the call button, ready to reignite the investigation, but the three faces looking back at me were not following.

'Surely, that's how we caught him,' said Barbie speaking slowly as if I was the one who was confused.

'When you went to bed, was the moon bright outside?'

She opened her mouth but then she got it. 'The moon wasn't on our side of the ship.'

'And the Prestwick Suite is arranged exactly the same as the Windsor. Niamh couldn't have seen the moon and probably couldn't have seen August because there was barely any light coming in through the windows.'

Alistair slapped his forehead. 'The sky was cloudy for a start, but out on the water, there is no light save for the moonlight and on the wrong side of the ship, it is utterly black.'

Jermaine asked. 'What does this mean, madam?'

Stabbing a finger at the phone, I said, 'It means we need to review the evidence.'

That Deepa Bhukari answered Lieutenant Baker's phone threw me for a moment. 'Deepa, we need to reopen the case,' I blurted.

It was two fifteen in the morning and the poor woman took a few seconds to get her brain into gear. 'What? Who? Is that you, Mrs Fisher? Sorry, I don't have my contacts in. I can't see the name on the screen.'

'Yes, it's Patricia. Is Martin there?'

I heard some whispering in the background and a moment of quiet before Lieutenant Baker's familiar Northern Irish twang filled my ear. 'Mrs Fisher?'

'Martin,' I used his first name since it was the middle of the night and he was in bed with his fiancée, 'Niamh Skies lied about seeing August leave the room last night.'

'What? She did what? How do you know?'

I explained about the moon and that it had been bothering me all day. There was something wrong and we needed to review the evidence.

'I don't know, Mrs Fisher. That's not a lot to go on.'

'We have to reopen the case. If Niamh Skies lied about seeing August, then we have to ask why.'

Baker sounded irritated when he replied, 'Well, why do you think she did, Mrs Fisher?'

'Think about it,' I urged. 'What is going to happen when the news of August's arrest and subsequent trial becomes public.'

In his cabin on the ship, probably sitting in the dark, Lieutenant Baker said, 'Um.'

'His fame and notoriety will increase tenfold. Have you ever heard that an artist's work increases exponentially in value once they are dead?'

'Yes. But he's not dead,' Baker pointed out.

'No,' I agreed. 'That's the bit that's bothering me.' The obvious answer as to why Niamh had lied about seeing August leave the suite with the murder weapon in his hand was that she was behind it and not him. I knew it couldn't be Evelyn, at least not for the second and third murders because she was in the brig at the time. However, Niamh could have done it. The question was why would she? If she was going to murder someone, why not murder August. As his wife she would inherit everything and the dead artist thing would kick in, making his art worth even more than it already was.

Sounding tired and a little annoyed, Baker asked, 'So what is it you wish to happen, Mrs Fisher? If we go back to review the evidence, what is it you want us to look for? What are you trying to find?'

Frustrated with myself because I was failing to articulate my concerns clearly enough, I said, 'Things that don't fit.' He was about to argue when I came at him from a different angle. 'The whole time I was looking at this case, I thought August was the one. When we look at the evidence with the killer already in our heads, we find ways to make what we are seeing fit our theories. We need to go back and look at it again with the viewpoint that he is innocent.'

'Innocent?' Lieutenant Baker almost choked. 'Mrs Fisher, are you serious?'

'This is on me,' I assured him. 'I got it wrong right at the start. I never really considered anyone else but the extra work you need to do now will stop an innocent man from going to jail.'

'So who did it?' Baker wanted to know.

I didn't have one slight clue.

When I admitted that, Baker said, 'I could understand Evelyn wanting Eoin dead. That's assuming the bruising Lieutenant Rudman said she saw was from Eoin hurting her and not a fall down the stairs.' I remembered the comment and how I had doubted her when Evelyn claimed he wasn't to blame for them. 'And if Niamh wanted Scarlet dead, why hadn't she done it ages ago. Her husband had been sleeping with other women since before she met him. Heck, she used to be one of them. Why would she target Scarlet?'

I didn't know the answer to that question either. Yet, somehow, I knew I was right. 'Can you do it?' I begged. 'Can you have another look at the evidence and let me know if anything stands out?'

He made a small sighing noise, but resigned to his fate, he said, 'Of course, Mrs Fisher. Keep your phone handy. I'll let you know what we find.'

With the call disconnected, I stared down at nothing much at all and wandered around inside my head for a moment. How had I made such a mess of this investigation? Sure, August Skies is a pig, but the more I thought about it, the less likely it seemed that he was the killer.

Putting the blood-stained trowel back into his toolbox? That was sloppy beyond belief. Anyone else would have tossed it over the side. The same could be said for the rag soaked in paint thinner. He uses it to ensure Vanessa is unconscious and then, with her DNA all over it, he puts it back into his toolbox where anyone investigating is bound to find it. And we had. And we'd believed it.

The whole case was a lie and I had willingly accepted everything the true killer had shown me. But who was the real killer?

Visitors

My sleep when I climbed back into bed was fitful and only came because I was so bone weary. Looking back at the last few days, I couldn't believe how little sleep I'd managed to amass. It was almost amazing that I hadn't simply fallen down at some point.

My phone rang at 0623hrs, jolting me awake as my arm shot out to snatch it from my nightstand. I didn't even look to see who the caller was because I felt convinced it had to be Lieutenant Baker.

I was wrong though, I got Schneider's thick Austrian accent instead. 'Mrs Fisher, we are trying to find you, but the address doesn't seem to match up to a house. There is just a driveway leading to a stately home in the distance.'

'It's not big enough to be a stately home,' I corrected him. 'It's a manor house.' Then what he said hit me. 'What do you mean? Are you outside?' I ran to the nearest window and threw the curtains open.

'It seemed simpler and more productive to bring the information to you,' Schneider replied.

'There is too much to share over the phone,' said Baker, his voice raised so I could hear it.

'I have you on speaker phone,' Schneider replied and there was an audible discussion where the Austrian tried to assure them they needed to go back to the big house and the rest of the voices in the car refused to believe anyone they knew could possibly live there.

Alistair was awake, eyeing me with a slightly fuzzy expression as he scratched his hair and smacked his lips together. 'Time to get up?'

'Your lieutenants are outside,' I told him, crossing the room at speed to snag my dressing gown again.

Two minutes later, Jermaine, who was somehow downstairs and already dressed in his butler's tails, opened the door to let our visitors in. The four security officers from the ship walked through the double wide, double height front entrance with looks of utter awe etched on their features.

'This is where you live?' asked Deepa Bhukari.

I shrugged in my embarrassment. 'The Maharaja gave it to me when I returned to England the last time. He said it no longer suited his needs.'

'Shall I prepare breakfast, madam?' asked Jermaine. It was a good thing we bought provisions the previous day though I wasn't sure we had enough to feed an extra five people. It turned out to be a moot point.

'I'm not sure we have time,' said Lieutenant Baker. 'You need to see what we have to show you.'

His bold claim sent us rushing to the kitchen where we could at least get tea while Baker and the others explained why they chose to jump in one of the cruise line's limousines and rush across the country.

'The police in Hampshire wouldn't let us see any of the evidence. They said the chain of evidence required that it remained sealed. It is to be handed over to the Garda in ...' he checked his watch. 'About half an hour. August Skies is being flown out of Heathrow on a ten o'clock flight to Dublin. That's the one bit of useful information we were able to get out of them. They were not interested in discussing the case.'

'Why not?' I asked incredulously.

'Because it's not their case,' Baker sighed, doing little to hide how frustrated he still was with their attitude.

'They were quite rude,' added Pippin. 'They didn't actually say it, but there was a definite suggestion that we should stop playing cop and go row a boat.'

We could deal with that later, right now I wanted to hear what they had found. 'If you couldn't get to the evidence, were you able to do anything?'

Lieutenant Baker placed his tablet on the table and turned it around so the screen faced me. 'We have photographs we took of the evidence and statements, nothing more. That, however, might be enough.'

On the screen was a photograph of the battery compartment on Evelyn's PDA. I had seen it before. Baker pointed to the batteries. 'I don't think any of us would ever have seen it if you hadn't asked us to look at it with a view to proving his innocence.'

Curious, but not seeing what he was trying to draw my attention to, I said, 'Okay.'

'The one thing that drove us to believe he was Vanessa's killer was the fingerprint on the battery, right?'

'Right,' I agreed.

'Why are there no prints on the PDA? We are testifying that he took his ex-wife's PDA and left a file on there which outlines how to kill Vanessa. It was the piece of evidence that would have convicted Evelyn and we were claiming he staged it to frame her. We can prove he is lying about never touching the device because we found his fingerprint inside it, where it would remain and never get accidentally wiped away or smudged.' He was making a good point, but not one that helped my argument that he was innocent.

Alistair nudged me. 'The batteries are different.'

I blinked. How could I have missed that? They weren't even the same brand. Then it hit me. August's blood sugar meter had been missing a battery and he went bananas about someone taking it. 'Oh, my God. The killer put the battery in there and trusted us to find it.'

Baker swiped the screen, speeding past other photographs to get to the next one he wanted, but stopped when I grabbed his arm.

'Go back,' I begged. Then did it myself for efficiency.

A photograph of the murder weapon appeared. The four-inch-long artist's trowel used to give depth and precision to his paintings bore the same blood stains I saw a day ago. Looking at it now, I saw what I failed to see before.

'That's not August's trowel.'

'How can you tell?' asked Alistair.

I looked down at the small steel object, the two sides coming together to make a sharply angled point, perfect for stabbing someone with. 'August shapes his. He has them made specially. I asked him about his paintings, and he went into great detail about how no one can achieve the same vivid mastery as he. His shaped trowel allows it. He also complained about how his wife ...' recalling his words exactly, I said, 'none of his women, ever paid the slightest attention to his work. I think he said it because I was the first to ask him about technique in years. That's not his trowel,' I repeated.

'Then it was planted,' said Alistair.

Baker pursed his lips. 'But by whom?'

There were other clues, other pieces of evidence which when questioned didn't necessarily add up the way I originally thought but the battery and the trowel were enough to remove all question from not only my mind, but that of Lieutenant Baker and everyone else around the table.

A flurry of motion followed because we now had a very small window to get to Heathrow airport if we wanted to speak with August again. He'd always denied any wrongdoing, and after they took him into custody yesterday morning, it never occurred to me to confront him about the truth again. I felt the case was closed and my mind had turned to other things such as leaving the suite and travelling home.

I was the guilty one - guilty of approaching the case with a closed mind.

I threw on clothes, trying to find something that matched, but between my depleted wardrobe and the clothes folded into several suitcases, I struggled, gave up, and ran from my bedroom wearing a summer dress over a pair of jeans, a coat in a colour that clashed rather than complemented, and running shoes because … well, because it was time for running.

Most everyone else was already downstairs by the time I got there, and cars were lined up ready to go. The task did not require that all of us went but no one wanted to be left behind. Tom the handyman would look after the dogs. He'd stayed behind at the house to keep it in good order while we were away and would continue to do so assuming I didn't now lose it in the divorce.

Instead of my Aston, we took the Overfinch Range Rover, a daft supercharged hybrid of a car that weighed the same as a bank vault and could get to sixty miles an hour faster than you could say it. Jermaine drove, his foot a little heavy on my instruction to get us there on time at all costs.

We would be running into London traffic on the godforsaken M25 motorway that circles the capital and is often referred to as a parking lot. It was only sixty miles to our destination so setting off before eight o'clock and defying the speed limit ought to have delivered us to our destination in plenty of time.

It didn't.

We split ourselves up between the cars, Lieutenant Baker jumping into my Range Rover along with Alistair which put Barbie in the limousine with the remaining three lieutenants. Baker called the police in Southampton, begging them to let him speak to August.

August had already been collected of course and the police were not interested in assisting us with any details – who were we to demand anything of them anyway? The Garda had August in custody, so our only hope was to catch them at the airport.

Not so easy when the traffic between you and your destination is bumper to bumper. The man in the driver's seat of the car next to me was reading his paper, so sure was he that we were not going to move any time soon.

I bit my nails and tapped my foot with impatience, all the while running different scenarios through my head. If I started with the assumption that August had killed no one, then I was left with only two persons from that party who could have. Everyone else was dead. Of the six on board, three were in the morgue, one was on his way to jail and that only left Evelyn and Niamh. I had already dismissed Evelyn because she was in the brig for the second two murders and could find no motive for her to kill the first victim, Vanessa.

Likewise Niamh, who had no reason that I could see to want Eoin and Scarlet dead.

The car's engine bursting back into life jerked me back to reality. 'We're moving?' I asked, eyes wide with hope.

In the driver's seat, Jermaine nodded. 'It looks that way, madam. I can see the cars ahead gathering speed.'

I leaned between the seats so I could see for myself and sure enough, half a mile ahead, the cars were starting to accelerate. I swear I held my breath until we were also cruising through the gears. Two minutes, and little more than a mile later, we passed a broken-down truck sitting on the hard shoulder and just beyond that, three cars in different states of wreck.

An accident. With so much weight of traffic converging into one space, it didn't take much to bring it all to a standstill. Now that we were moving again, the cars ate up the miles and soon we were seeing signs for Heathrow with dwindling mileages posted. At nine o'clock, it looked like we might make it, that was until we found another couple of sticky spots.

Lieutenant Baker believed the flight was at ten and I knew they would begin boarding half an hour before that. Terminal two serves flights to Ireland but even knowing which building we wanted, we still needed to find which flight they were on and get to them. I genuinely believed we were sunk but had to keep going regardless.

As we reached the departure building, Jermaine was forced to reduce his speed for the slow-moving traffic and posted speed limits.

'Bail?' asked Baker, one hand already on his door handle.

'Bail,' I agreed, and Jermaine barely got to stop the car before Baker, Alistair and I leapt from it. Craning my head when I heard shouts behind, I was relieved to see it wasn't airport security chasing us, but Barbie, Pippin, and Bhukari.

At the giant board listing all the departures, six of us skidded to a stop. My eyes were wild, trying to find the flight we wanted.

'There!' shouted Pippin, pointing his arm. 'It's an Air Ireland flight!'

He took off running, getting three paces before Deepa shouted, 'We have to buy tickets to get through security to the gates, dummy!'

The fact that the Maharaja of Zangrabar had chosen to be my benefactor puts me in a financially comfortable position. The fact that his generosity makes me uncomfortable probably tells you volumes about me. Regardless, the third richest person on the planet picks up most of my bills so I have money of my own that I don't need, and I gladly handed over my credit card to buy eight tickets to Dublin. Two of them I was leaving at the desk assuming Jermaine and Schneider would catch up once they ditched the cars.

'Which gate?' I asked, knowing the plane was due to take off soon.

The lady in her lovely emerald green uniform said, 'Gate twenty-three.'

Pippin, possibly a little over excited by it all, shouted, 'Gate twenty-three!' then charged into the distance with everyone hot on his heels.

The lady serving me had a questioning look on her face. I cringed and said, 'They are very excited to go to Dublin.'

'Well, they needn't rush,' she replied in her lovely Irish accent. 'The flight just got delayed by half an hour.'

I allowed myself a wry smile as my friends vanished into the crowd of people filling the airport. Having abandoned me, Alistair would soon realise and return looking sheepish no doubt. I could have shouted but making myself heard over the public address system announcements and the chatter of thousands of people seemed impossible, so I sauntered nonchalantly after them instead.

If you have never been there, let me tell you, Heathrow airport is big. I've heard it said that Heathrow is the biggest airport in the world. Now, I don't know if that is true, but it sure felt like it at that moment.

No doubt, for people who are familiar with the place, it is easy to navigate, but I had to scout around until I found a sign, only to then realise the signs were so big and obvious I had been ignoring them.

Alistair didn't come back for me, but he did look sheepish when I found him.

'Where did you get to, darling?' he asked, sounding genuinely concerned. 'I thought you were right beside me, but when we arrived at the gate you were nowhere in sight.'

'Yes, dear, you left me behind,' I replied, being cruel but grinning cheekily so he knew I was just teasing.

My focus wasn't on my gorgeous boyfriend but on Lieutenant Baker who was locked in a heated discussion with several men in Garda uniform. I liked that Alistair was prepared to stand back and let his security team handle it, rather than wading in himself just because he was here.

Seeing me looking, Alistair said, 'They are refusing to allow us access to their prisoner.' It didn't come as that much of a shock to me. 'They are here to escort him back to Ireland, and in their words, "Are not trying to solve a mystery."'

I didn't know how often suspects are transferred on commercial flights – I figured it wasn't something that would normally be necessary. In these circumstances, where the distance and the time it would take overland made that option impractical, a commercial flight made perfect sense. It's not as if the prison system had money lying around to hire private jets.

That the Garda officers were here to perform a simple task and had no desire nor need to complicate it was no surprise, but I needed to speak to August, and I had to at least try to make the Garda officers listen.

I approached them. At the gate where the aircraft which ought to be outside was conspicuously absent, the Garda and their prisoner were positioned in one corner with a large, invisible exclusion zone around them. August, wearing a pale blue all-in-one jumpsuit was handcuffed and wearing ankle manacles. I felt bad seeing him like that for even though I knew he was a narcissistic pig, he wasn't a killer, and it was my fault the world now thought he was.

Sitting on one of a line of plastic chairs, he had a burly-looking Garda officer sitting on his left hand side and another standing just a foot or so to his left. Five yards in front of them, two more Garda officers were making sure no one came near the prisoner.

The remaining passengers – doing a rough head count, I had to assume the plane was half full or less – were packed into the other half of the waiting area for the gate.

The two officers keeping everyone back were focussed on Lieutenant Baker, who had on his left and right, his colleagues Deepa Bhukari and

Anders Pippin. I could see how frustrated my friends were getting long before I got near enough to hear the discussion.

'The prisoner travels back to Ireland,' one of the Garda officers said. It was clear it wasn't the first time he had said it. 'There is no other outcome that can happen.'

Baker had clearly gone around this conversation more than once too and was trying a new approach. 'What happens once he is on Irish soil then? We need to reinterview him and reopen our case.'

'Too late,' the officer replied. His voice was calm and unflustered but also determined with an unwavering edge; an experienced man doing a job that ought to be simple if the annoying ship's security would just go away. 'The prisoner is now in our custody. His innocence or guilt will be proven one way or the other by Garda officers and he will be tried in accordance with Irish law. For the last time, sir, move away, or I shall have airport security remove you and your colleagues.'

'Do you recognise me?' I asked. Both Garda officers twitched their heads to look my way and I saw them connect my face to the pictures they must have seen on television or in the newspapers. 'This is my fault,' I admitted.

Behind them, August Skies had finally looked up from staring at the floor and he was trying to get to his feet. A strong hand on his shoulder kept him in place.

When he shouted something obscene, the two Garda officers facing me, turned to look briefly, but soon had their eyes back in my direction.

'I messed up. August didn't kill anyone. I just need to speak with him, please. A few answers will clear up the gaps in what I know, and I will be able to present the real killer. You don't have to set him free; I know you can't do that, but just a minute of conversation is all I need.'

The nearest Garda officer was the one who had spoken previously. He leaned forward at the waist, keeping his eyes locked on mine. Then, with a lot of emphasis, he said, 'No,' and straightened again.

I nodded. He didn't have to do anything to help, I got that, but his lousy attitude surprised me. I had no option, so I said, 'Thank you,' and backed away a pace. The lieutenants looked surprised, but came with me, following as I backed away with my eyes locked on August's.

Once I was far enough away from the Garda officers, I drew in a deep breath and shouted, 'August, who stands to benefit from your incarceration?' Everyone in our section of the terminal heard me. August certainly did. 'I know you didn't do it,' I added.

The two Garda officers with August were moving to block my view of him and urgently giving him instructions which were probably cautions not to answer me. The other two officers were coming in my direction, but they were met with a wall of resistance as Baker, Pippin, and Bhukari formed a human shield swiftly joined by Alistair and Barbie, and then Schneider and Jermaine who had ditched the cars somewhere and tracked us down.

Alistair addressed the Garda officers. 'It would be simpler to let her speak with your prisoner. She's going to do it anyway.'

As it turned out, that was the wrong thing to say because airport security arrived, assessed the situation in a heartbeat and gave the Garda and their prisoner another area to wait in until the flight was ready to board.

Once they were out of sight, I slumped into a chair. 'I guess I'm going back to Dublin then.'

A sense of Déjà Vu gripped me as we boarded the plane. I was going back to Dublin, a place I had never visited until two days ago but somehow was now flying back to as if I had left something important there and needed to return to collect it.

Why were we even going? Okay, I had to shell out for tickets just so we could get to the gate, but that didn't mean we had to get on the flight. What could I do when we got there? I was still trying to figure that out as I settled into my seat.

The lieutenants had not come with us. They needed to return to the Aurelia at speed or they would miss its departure, so it was Alistair and me with Barbie and Jermaine who were going on what might prove to be a fruitless trip to Ireland.

Landing in Dublin, August would be taken from the airport under guard and loaded into a prisoner transport van or perhaps just a police car. Either way, I wasn't going to be able to do anything to change the attitude we had already faced. So what then? At best I could go to the Garda headquarters, wherever that was, and plead my case. Maybe they would let me speak to August tomorrow.

But it hit me then that I had been going about this the wrong way and a sneaking glimpse of the truth flashed at me from a dark corner of my brain.

With frantic hands, I grabbed at the handbag already tucked away beneath my seat. Grabbing my phone, I opened the contacts list and dialled the one number I had for a person who might very well be able to change my fortune.

'Sorry, madam. No calls allowed once the plane is in motion,' a lady air steward chided.

I put the phone away obediently, then whipped it out again the moment she moved on. The call failed to connect – of course it did because it was my last-ditch Hail Mary throw – so I sent a text message instead and settled back into my seat as the force of the accelerating aircraft pushed me into it.

Theories

The flight from Heathrow to Dublin is a short hop. Barely ninety minutes in the air so by the time the plane levels off, the pilot is already thinking about coming back down. I was tired and worried I would simply fall asleep if I closed my eyes, but I was also wired with energy and frantically trying to unpick the mystery in my head.

I couldn't talk to August, so I was going to have to work this out by myself. The confusion I had all centred around who could have killed the three victims and what they gained by doing so. Unless I chose to invent a new person in this tragedy, the only people who could be guilty were Evelyn and Niamh. I knew Niamh had lied about seeing August in the moonlight and I knew someone had been trying to frame August, planting the trowel used to murder Eoin and Scarlet in his toolbox and the paint thinner soaked rag used to subdue Vanessa too.

But then if that was true, someone had also been trying to frame Evelyn for Vanessa's murder, planting the detailed plan for how to kill her on Evelyn's PDA. If I asked who would want to frame Evelyn, I got no answer at all, but whoever it was tried to make her look guilty while also planting the battery from August's blood sugar meter in the PDA to make us think he was the one trying to frame her.

Honestly, it was making my head hurt.

What if Niamh was the killer? I tried that on for size, but she had an ironclad alibi for Vanessa's death, and I had no proof she ever left her suite during the night. In contrast, I knew August was roaming the passageways because Lady Mary spotted him. Niamh lied to implicate August though. Why would she do that?

August's toolbox wasn't locked so anyone could have put something in it. That wasn't true though because it couldn't be just anyone. The people with access to it was a very small pool which, once I eliminated the dead people, took me back to Evelyn and Niamh.

In theory, either one could have planted the evidence in his toolbox of artist's bits, and either one could have popped the battery out of his blood sugar meter. Evelyn wouldn't have framed herself though, so that left Niamh who I knew hadn't killed Vanessa.

Frowning and huffing, and ignoring Alistair when he asked if I was okay, I cleared my mind and tried again from a new angle: why would Evelyn frame herself?

The only answer I could come up with was so that she would be in the brig and have a perfect alibi for the murder of her boyfriend and his lover. My skull itched and I froze, capturing the theory that just ran through my head and narrowing in on it.

When thirty seconds later, the answer hit me like an uppercut to the jaw, I squealed in shock loud enough to make Alistair spill his coffee and scare the lady from the flight crew who poured hot black liquid onto the carpet.

Shaking his hand to get the scalding coffee from his fingers, Alistair turned to look at me in the cramped space. 'Patricia?'

I was quivering with nervous energy. I was right. I was utterly convinced of it, but it made the need for my text message to have been received and understood even more vital than it had been before. If I was right, and this time I felt sure I was, then we were dealing with a level of cold-bloodedness I had never before witnessed. Even Verity Tuppence, overlord of a criminal empire, might think twice about doing what I believed had been done.

I pushed myself up in my chair, craning my neck to look back down the plane to where the last three rows and the toilet at that end had been cordoned off. The Garda officers brought August onto the plane before the rest of us were allowed entry. Would it be reversed in Dublin? Standard passengers getting off first to clear the route for the dangerous criminal? That was what I needed.

The captain announced the flight's descent into Dublin and in doing so let me know that I was going to find out soon enough.

A Favour Returned

Not for the first time in the last few days, fate chose to get in my way. The Garda officers must have called ahead because they were met by a fresh contingent of reinforcements who boarded the plane to augment their colleagues' numbers.

Over the tannoy, the pilot requested that all passengers remain in their seats until cleared to leave. He didn't say it was so the prisoner could be extracted first but that was what it was for.

'What's happening, Patty?' asked Barbie, leaning across the aisle. 'I heard you squeal.'

I puffed out my cheeks and bit my tongue, unsure what to say at this point. 'I think I've worked it out,' I told her, though Alistair and Jermaine were listening too.

Her eyebrows shot upward. 'You've figured out who killed Vanessa, Eoin, and Scarlet?'

I nodded. 'I think so.' I was certain I had but didn't want to get cocky.

'Was it Evelyn?' Barbie asked.

I shook my head.

Alistair frowned. 'Niamh?'

I shook my head again.

Jermaine leaned around Barbie. 'Madam, if it was neither of those, who does that leave?'

With a shark's smile and a waggle of my eyebrows, I gave them a cryptic answer, 'I didn't say it was neither of them.'

My three companions all exchanged confused looks but before they could jab me with a verbal or physical finger, the pilot announced we could depart, and I was on my feet and moving the next second. With no baggage beyond my handbag, I was able to slip through the gaps as other passengers fished in the overhead lockers and was running down the mobile stairs even as the flight steward yelled after me to walk not run.

My companions had no trouble keeping pace, each of them fitter and more physically capable than me, but as it turned out, I hadn't needed to rush at all.

At the edge of the tarmac as it met the terminal building two Garda vans were parked. They were there to transport the prisoner and the eight officers to wherever they were going next. However, though they had reached their vehicles well ahead of us, none of them were getting in yet and I could see the reason why.

'Hello, Mrs Fisher,' said Inspector Meanan, stepping forward to greet me.

'Thank you so much for getting here in time,' I breathed a sigh of relief as I shook his hand and felt like pulling him into a hug. I quickly introduced him to Alistair, Barbie, and Jermaine, but I was interrupted before I could say anything more.

'Sir, we need to move the prisoner to holding and process him,' stated the same Garda officer who did all the talking back at Heathrow.

Inspector Meanan shot his head around so fast his eyes must have rattled. I couldn't see his expression now that he was facing away from me, but it must have been fierce because six of the eight officers took a step back.

'Do I outrank you?' Inspector Meanan demanded to know.

Glued to the spot, the officer did his best to argue. 'Yes, sir, but protocol dictates ...'

'Blast your protocol, man. Mrs Fisher wishes to speak with your prisoner and that is what is going to happen.' Inspector Meanan turned back around to face me, his face fixed with a warm smile once more. 'I am glad I was able to return the favour I owed you so swiftly, Mrs Fisher.'

'Call me Patricia, please,' I begged, then pulled a grimace of sorts as I changed the request I originally made in my text message. 'Actually, I just have the one question for him, Inspector.'

'You must call me, Fionn,' the inspector insisted, and we were now on first name terms. He didn't even look at his officers when he ordered, 'Bring the prisoner forward.'

August was eyeing me warily, not that I blamed him. However, I wanted to believe he could see I had chased him across a sea to fix my mistake when I could have easily chosen to leave him to rot.

'August, where is your artwork stored?' I asked.

The question caught him by surprise, and though he was cautious in giving his answer, he revealed the location anyway, 'Outside of Portmarnock on the coast. I have a workshop there. Why?'

I turned my attention away from the artist to chance my luck with the Garda. It was a good thing Inspector Meanan was on my side. 'Inspector, we need to go to his workshop. Directly,' I added, just in case they didn't understand the urgency.

'Sir, I really must protest,' started the talkative Garda officer.

A raised hand from Inspector Meanan was all it required to stop him mid-flow. The senior officer eyed me sceptically. 'I owe you, Mrs Fisher, and I trust your judgement given some of the reports I have read in the paper. However, I would like a little more to go on than your word. Can you do that for me?'

'Can I explain on the way?'

The long Route to the Truth

I was thankful to discover that Portmarnock, which I had never heard of, was but a short drive from the airport. Less than fifteen minutes in fact though it took a little longer to get to his workshop which overlooked the sea.

On the way, and because Barbie among others would throttle me if I didn't explain, I laid out my thoughts.

'August Skies is famous for two things. Firstly, he is a talented artist sought after by the rich and famous. He could charge whatever he wants for his work but that takes us neatly to the second point because he refuses to charge them anything.

Inspector Meanan shot me a quizzical look.

I did my best to explain. 'August Skies refuses to take payment, surviving by bartering his work for that which he wants instead of money. Some might say he is bonkers. I would certainly call him eccentric. The cruise aboard the Aurelia was in exchange for painting several newly commissioned works for the cruise line. He gets housed, fed and watered in the lap of luxury for several months and all he has to do is slap some paint on a few canvases.'

It was probably a good thing at this point that August was travelling in the Garda police van behind us and thus unable to hear my opinion. Inspector Meanan was driving his car, having kicked his driver out to fit me and my three friends in and there was no room for anyone else.

I knew I was oversimplifying August's talent but doing so wasn't going to affect the outcome of the case. With everyone waiting for me to get to the point, I continued. 'August has a third feature for which he is less well known. He maintains a womanising, playboy lifestyle even though he is nearing seventy. Married twice and still married to the second of them, he takes in attractive young women wherever he can and calls them his muses. They are not paid, but then neither are his wives, and his ex-wife, Evelyn Skies, told me how badly she got stung in the divorce. August has no net worth so she can have half but what is that worth to her?'

It was a rhetorical question, of course.

Inspector Meanan felt it was time to hurry me along. 'You said three people had been killed?'

He was prompting me to explain why we were going to August's workshop and why I felt certain he was not the killer. I knew I was dragging it out, but to understand, they would have to take the same long road I had to travel to arrive at the truth.

'August has a history of violence towards his women when provoked.' I got an uncomfortable look from the inspector. 'He was convicted and has several out of court settlements, I believe. That's not really a factor in this, it just helps to know that when we get to the end. You see August is blind to just about everything except his art and his women, but he doesn't really care about the women in his life. They are just things to him. In the same way that he eschews money, he avoids any real emotional commitment by always having several women on the go.'

'Sounds like he's a lot cleverer than I expected,' joked the inspector dryly.

I ignored the comment to press on. 'The thing is his women never really cared about him either. Evelyn thought she would be the rich wife of a famous artist. She was young when they married, and he was already established. She put up with the womanising but when he pushed her out, replacing her with a younger model, Niamh, she turned vengeful, aiming to clean him out in the divorce. She got nothing as I already told you and had to come crawling back to him.'

Alistair said, 'Patricia, dear, you are painting the man you believe to be innocent very much as the bad guy.'

I had to concede his point. 'He is a bad person. However, being unpleasant, arrogant, conceited, and narcissistic are not crimes. Evelyn knew more about him than anyone else, so she became his manager/promoter/marketing person. She got to stay close to him but that also put her back in the toxic environment which Niamh now ruled. The two clashed and that is one of the reasons it took me so long to work it all out.'

'Work what out, Patty?' begged Barbie, squeezed in next to me on the back seat.

Okay, I'd given them almost enough preamble. 'Evelyn met someone new.'

'Eoin Planchet,' Jermaine supplied.

'That's right. Eoin Planchet, a steroid-abusing, muscle-bound freak who beat her or hurt her on a regular basis.'

'I didn't know that,' said Barbie, horrified by the idea.

I gave her an honest face. 'I don't know it for certain either. Lieutenant Rudman said she saw bruises all over Evelyn's body that would be consistent with getting knocked about regularly. Given his size, he wouldn't have to exert much force to hurt her.'

'Are you suggesting she killed Eoin?' asked Barbie. 'She was in the brig.'

'That's right,' I agreed. 'That's why Niamh did it for her.' Silence ruled in the car as the other people in it tried to absorb what I had just told them. 'We know Niamh could not have killed Vanessa and we know Evelyn could not have killed Eoin and Scarlet. And we also know Evelyn and Scarlet couldn't be in it together because they hate each other.'

Everyone was looking at me, even Inspector Meanan which meant he wasn't looking at the road. When a car horn blared, he swore and wrestled the steering wheel for a second. As his heart rate returned to normal, he asked, 'Anyone else confused?'

I chuckled. 'Don't you see? The reason none of it made sense was because we were sold a lie right at the start. Alistair and I heard wife and ex-wife arguing fiercely when we arrived back at the quayside. Then Barbie and I saw Niamh and Evelyn exchanging insults. We were supposed to see those things.'

Alistair shook his head in disbelief. 'You're saying it was staged?'

'Both women have more than one problem. In Evelyn's case, she had a boyfriend who hurts her, and she can no more escape him than she can the company of her ex-husband and his harem because she had no money. None to speak of anyway. Far too little to escape to a new life. Two problems. Niamh has two problems of her own. She also has no money but why would she want to escape? Because she thinks August is going to do to her exactly what he did to Evelyn and replace her with Vanessa.'

'But you told us August didn't seem to care about Vanessa dying,' Barbie pointed out.

'Yes. I didn't say her concerns were justified.'

'And wasn't Vanessa about to run away with someone called B?' asked Jermaine.

I shook my head. 'Sadly not. How many times did you call the number for B, trying to raise him?' I asked both Jermaine and Barbie.

They exchanged a glance. 'Fifty, wasn't it?' Barbie asked.

'What if I told you Evelyn's phone was going nuts all night in its locker in the brig? She couldn't get to it and Lieutenant Rudman didn't answer it.'

Jermaine gasped. 'Evelyn Skies was B?'

'It took me forever to figure that part out,' I admitted sadly. 'I had to scrap everything I thought I knew and come at it from the one angle that couldn't possibly be true. I could only figure it out if the two women who clearly hated each other were actually working together. They planned to end all their problems in one go. Evelyn killed Vanessa. Vanessa took drugs recreationally, so it probably wasn't hard for Evelyn to convince her to have some with her. Or maybe Evelyn had none and just poured the champagne. She murdered the girl on behalf of Niamh, carefully framing August for the crime. The whole thing with B was a ruse to make whoever investigated the case believe August had discovered the relationship or Vanessa's intention to leave and lashed out angrily as he had in the past.'

Barbie gave me a horrified look. 'But that means ... oh, wow. They set this up weeks and weeks ago, luring Vanessa into a relationship with a person who never existed just so they could murder her and frame August.'

Alistair frowned so deeply his eyebrows almost touched his cheeks. 'But she didn't frame August. Evelyn had the note on her PDA to tell us how *she* performed the murder. You said the battery in her device was from August's blood sugar meter but why incriminate herself at all?'

'Because she had to have the alibi. Being in the brig made sure she was out of the frame for the next killings and they had to make sure August wasn't looked at for Vanessa because if we'd zeroed in on him instantly, they wouldn't be able to frame him for Eoin and Scarlet's deaths.'

Barbie saw it, her jaw dropping open. 'We had to figure it out at the right time, or they couldn't pull it off.'

I nodded. 'That's right. Niamh needed a reason to pretend to hit the bottle. She probably had some of the whiskey but faked drinking the rest. She made everyone think she was drunk but how hard is that? She stunk of whiskey but all she had to do was spill some down herself. She was drinking in plain sight, but do we actually know it was whiskey in the bottle?'

Alistair shook his head ruefully. 'When you put it like that, it's like a magician's trick. They fool you by making you look where they want your eyes to be, which is not where the trick is performed.'

I nodded, still angry with myself for being fooled so easily. 'Niamh played the role of a wife lying to defend her husband perfectly. I expect they had a clever plan to make sure we found out August was out of his room that night, but they didn't need to enact it because I found out through Lady Mary. Niamh sent her husband to get her painkillers, slipped from the room right after him and went straight to Scarlet's cabin.'

'Wait,' said Barbie. 'I thought Scarlet was in Eoin's cabin?'

I shook my head. 'I think Eoin was telling us the truth when he said he didn't like Scarlet. They weren't lovers, at least I don't believe they were. Yet again, Evelyn and Niamh needed the finger to point to August. If we believed his young muse was cheating on him, essentially rejecting him for another man, then we would assume he killed them both in a fit of jealousy.'

'Which we did,' admitted Jermaine.

'Which I did,' I corrected him. 'I couldn't see anything beyond my desire for the horrible man to be guilty. I found the clues that would fit my desire, the clues so neatly and carefully left by his wife and ex-wife. They made mistakes though. The battery they took with his fingerprint on didn't match the other battery in Evelyn's PDA. That would have been easy to fix just by buying more batteries to match the one from August's machine and we never would have checked it. They could have put one of the batteries into his blood sugar meter and no one would ever have known it was missing. Then there was the trowel.'

Inspector Meanan shot me a questioning look because he knew nothing about any of this.

I explained. 'Artists sometimes use a small trowel to apply paint. It gives the ability to merge the paint and create textures otherwise not possible. August claimed to be the best in the world. Perhaps he is, but the point is he had his trowels specially made with a crescent shape along the right hand edge. He says the shape is the key to using it with the accuracy he achieves. The trowel used to kill Eoin and Scarlet, the one we subsequently found in his toolbox has no crescent. If we ignore how incredibly sloppy it would be to put the murder weapon where we were bound to find it, given that we are supposed to believe he went to the trouble of trying to frame Evelyn for Vanessa's murder, why would he use a trowel that wasn't even one of his?'

Nobody offered an answer until Alistair said, 'He wouldn't.'

I agreed. 'No, I don't think he would. In his toolbox we found physical evidence to tie him to the murders. We were supposed to believe he killed three people, while the real killers hid behind perfect alibis.'

'So this was all about getting revenge?' asked Inspector Meanan.

'Revenge, yes, in part. But revenge would only deal with one of their problems.' I could smell the ocean now, and the landscape was changing, the horizon in front of us no longer containing as much land as it had. In the next moment, the land dipped down a little to reveal the dark waves and the ocean stretching into the distance. White tips rippled along the wave crests.

Alistair answered the question I hadn't asked. 'They would still have no money.'

'And that's where the art comes in.'

Inspector Meanan turned a corner, leaned forward to see if he was in the right place, and pulled off the main road to take a narrow side street. 'You think the two women are after his artwork? What? They'll sell it because he's in jail and can't stop them until it's too late?'

I shrugged. 'It makes sense to me. At this point they think they have gotten away clean. August is on his way to jail and no one is looking at them. Evelyn has been managing his commissions for years, chances are she has buyers set up already.'

Inspector Meanan swung the steering wheel, crossing the road to enter a driveway covered in drifting sand. Overgrown gorse bushes grew all around, obscuring the property but when I saw cars and a van, I knew we were in the right place.

'How are you going to prove this, Patty?' Barbie wanted to know.

Two women stepped out from behind the van, chatting in an animated way with a man in a fine suit.

Nodding my head at familiar faces, I said, 'Let's ask them, shall we?'

Change of Venue

My right hand held Alistair's left where he sat next to me, and in my left hand, a cold glass of rhubarb and ginger gin and tonic slowly warmed, the ice cubes melting while I stared at the darkening sky through my tiny window. It would be fully dark by the time we touched back down in Heathrow, and from there we still needed to get home. It already felt like a long day.

If I closed my eyes, I knew I would be asleep in seconds, but I didn't want to sleep. Not yet. I would snuggle up next to Alistair tonight in the big bed in my big house and I wouldn't have niggling doubts about a case to keep me awake.

The van outside August's workshop displayed the livery of a large and world-famous London auction house. I knew from seeing articles on television that they had been entrusted with selling off works by Picasso, Monet, and Rembrandt to name just three.

The term bang to rights had popped into my head again as we approached the two women though I chose not to employ it. Evelyn and Niamh froze when they saw the Garda uniforms, then tried to run, which was good enough for me as a declaration of guilt.

Inspector Meanan knew everything I knew. Or perhaps that should be everything I suspected. Either way, the case was his now, his personal involvement would make it hard for him to pass to anyone else and why would he want to? The press would be all over it, sticking a fine feather in his cap when the convictions were brought.

August didn't get released which was a shame, but they let me make a personal apology to him which he seemed to begrudgingly accept. I expected he would be out by the morning and wondered whether he would fall back into his old ways of luring attractive young women to his bed.

Apparently, I fell asleep anyway, because the next thing I knew, Alistair was waking me, my drink was gone, and the plane was coming in to land.

Jermaine had thrown the car into the first car park he found but in the sprawling mass of Heathrow, it took us a while to find it again. The dark descending didn't help. Coming up to it, a figure suddenly emerged from the dark, startling me until I saw who it was.

'Martin?'

Alistair sucked in a breath of surprise. 'Lieutenant Baker.' Pippin, Schneider, and Bhukari also stepped out from the dark. 'I hate to state the obvious, but you are not on the ship,' Alistair pointed out.

All four of them looked miserably remorseful. 'We hit traffic, sir. We missed it,' admitted Baker, his head hung in shame.

I felt terrible. Crew failing to get back to the ship in time for its departure was an instant dismissal event in many cases. If that happened to them, it would be because they answered my call for help. I got them into this.

Alistair sucked in a hard, thoughtful breath through his nose. 'I think a call to Purple Star will fix this. Extenuating circumstances and all that. No. Better yet, you are all on two weeks holiday which started yesterday. I will speak with Captain Stubbs in the morning. This was my omission, not yours and that is how it will be recorded.' Alistair was going to falsify the records to protect his crew. Goodness me I was in love with him.

Lieutenant Baker and his three colleagues all glanced at each other. 'Sir, I don't know what to say,' Baker stammered.

Alistair frowned at him. 'For a start, you can explain what you are doing in uniform while on shore leave?' he demanded an answer in a tone that would make a person want to run away and hide. However, when his face split into a big grin, they knew he was having some fun at their expense. 'I take it you have nowhere to stay and are still in possession of a limousine.'

'Yes, sir,' admitted Lieutenant Baker.

Alistair nodded. 'Jolly good. I think perhaps you should follow us back to Kent.' Alistair squeezed my hand and looked down at me for confirmation.

I laughed. 'We have plenty of space. You absolutely must come with us.'

Cringing, Baker raised his hand. 'Sorry. Just one minor problem with all this, sir.' Alistair raised one eyebrow. 'Lieutenant Bhukari and I are due to get married next weekend, sir. You were to perform the ceremony. On the ship.'

Alistair nodded. 'That is a pickle. It will be difficult to show you didn't miss the ship's departure because you were on leave already while I forgot to file, if you then go back to the ship to get married and thus prove you were supposed to be there the whole time.' Deepa came to stand next to her fiancé. Alistair scratched his chin. 'How about this? You have some family coming, yes?'

Lieutenant Bhukari said, 'Mine live in England, sir. In Preston.'

'Mine are from Ballykinloss in Northern Ireland, sir,' said Baker.

'Would you accept a change of venue? Could you be convinced to perform your nuptials here in England instead?'

The young couple looked at each other, both searching the other's face for any sign of what they might feel about the sudden, but probably necessary change of plans.

Deepa broke the silence first, reaching out to take Martin's hand, she said, 'I don't care where it is, as long as I get you.'

Martin kissed her quickly, a peck on the lips before turning his face back to his captain with a broad smile across it. 'We will need a venue, sir.'

Alistair slowly turned his gaze in my direction, a wolfish grin spreading from one side of his face to the other. 'I have just the place in mind,' he revealed, making me frown with curiosity because as far as I knew, he didn't know anywhere here. 'I hear Loxton Hall is a wonderful place for a wedding.'

The End

(Except it isn't. There is a lot more to come, and much more available. Scroll down to see)

Author's notes:

Dublin in Ireland has been on my list of places to visit for a long time. I guess I will get there eventually, but since it is not a very child-oriented destination – the kids would be bored with dad touring the Guinness factory for two hours – it will stay on the backburner for a while. During my twenty-five years in the British Army, it was on the list of places I needed to seek special permission to visit – all due to 'the troubles' and the Irish Republican Army and other factions all wanting to kill British soldiers.

I didn't bother to seek the permission needed, nor did I risk just going as I am certain many of my brethren did. Nevertheless, it was fun taking virtual tours and scouring maps to get a feel for the place as I researched this book.

My wife has several Irish friends from the teaching community, among which is a Niamh. They come to England for jobs. If you struggled with her name, you are not alone. I called one of my wife's friends Nerm for ages having read her name before I heard it. Much like Americans and English, to name just two nations who speak English, we have different words for the same thing. The Irish go one better, much like the Welsh, to have utterly confusing ways of spelling words. To me it seems that sometimes none of the letters when they say it are actually used when they write it.

Now that I have insulted at least one complete nation of people, I'll think I'll leave the subject alone.

Patricia's nineteenth outing had to pick up from the glorious conclusion to the Godmother storyline and begin to forge a new chapter in her life. Now firmly ensconced in Alistair's life, the romance, will-they-won't-they subplot also ends so it's a good thing I have new ideas to tie the next ten or so books together.

Patricia book twenty will be along very soon. But if you are not reading this note from me a few days after this book was released then it is almost certainly already waiting for you. Chances are several more are too.

As I finish off this note, I have a Christmas tree twinkling away just a yard or so from my left elbow. My five-year-old son has just one day left in school before he breaks up for the holidays and I may need a piece of rope to tether him to the Earth he is that high with excitement.

We are in full COVID lock down still with no sign of it abating. Indeed, the virus here is believed to have mutated so a more virulent, faster-spreading version is now terrorising the south of England. I remain safely squirreled away in my house writing books for you to read, but outside, people take their lives in their hands just to get bread and milk.

It will be a strange, party-free, relative-free, visitor-free Christmas and I am thankful I have a family to share it with for I know so many will be by themselves. My mother is one of them, but I dare not visit her, or bring her to my house for fear my son, attending one of the very few schools in the area still open, might be unwittingly carrying the virus. The exact same applies to my mother-in-law.

I think that will do for now. I need to get this book away to be read by my team of willing volunteers. They do their best to root out all the spelling and grammar errors my flying fingers introduce and provide feedback on the story in general. Next, I will be visiting Arbroath in Scotland with Rex and Albert as they get into all manner of bother trying to track the elusive Gastrothief.

Take care.

Steve Higgs

What's next for Patricia Fisher?

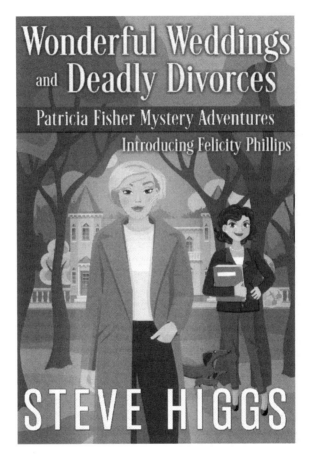

Wonderful Weddings and Deadly Divorces

Patricia Fisher Mystery Adventures

Introducing Felicity Phillips

STEVE HIGGS

Back in England for a brief visit with boyfriend Alistair in tow, there's just enough time for Patricia and friends to get into trouble.

She's got the whole gang with her as they go all out to organise a fast wedding – such a shame it's at the same venue Angelica Howard-Box is using for her son's nuptials.

As the fur starts to fly, a body is found, and it just might be that Patricia's nemesis needs her help.

It's going to be a wild ride for sure and there's the small matter of Patricia's divorce to finalise. Will Charlie get his way and steal her fortune? Or is Patricia just a little bit cleverer than his entire team of lawyers?

Find out in Wonderful Weddings and Deadly Divorces

A FREE Rex and Albert Story

There is no catch. There is no cost. You won't even be asked for an email address. I have a FREE Rex and Albert short story for you to read simply because I think it is fun and you deserve a cherry on top. If you have not yet already indulged, please click the picture below and read the fun short story about Rex and Albert, a ring and a Hellcat.

When a former police dog knows the cat is guilty, what must he do to prove his case to the human he lives with?

His human is missing a ring. The dog knows the cat is guilty. Is the cat smarter than the pair of them?

A home invader. A thief. A cat. Is that one being or three? The dog knows but can he make his human listen?

Baking. It can get a guy killed.

On a culinary tour of the British Isles, retired Detective Superintendent Albert Smith and snarky former police dog Rex Harrison find something quite unexpected waiting for them at their B&B ...

... it's the almost dead body of their landlady.

Refusing to believe in coincidence, Albert and Rex set out to discover why her 'accident' is the second terrible event there in two days. Something is stirring in Bakewell and it's not the ingredients for a famous tart.

In trouble faster than a souffle can fall, the duo must work fast before anyone else has an accident. But the landlady's twin sister is hiding a secret, Albert keeps calling it a tart when it's a pudding, and their taxi driver, Asim, appears to use a language all of his own.

With Rex's nose working overtime, you can be sure they'll track down the bad guys responsible. Unfortunately, that might be when the real trouble begins.

AMANDA HARPER
PARANORMAL
DETECTIVE
BLUE MOON INVESTIGATIONS BOOK THREE
STEVE HIGGS

Am I going to get my soul sucked out by a malevolent spirit? That's what BFF and former police colleague Patience thinks will happen.

My name is Amanda Harper, and I am a paranormal detective with the Blue Moon Investigation Agency. As of today, that is, and my first case is at the local shopping mall where terrified shoppers hysterically claim a ghost attacked them in the elevators. Not just one elevator – all of them.

Sounds like an easy enough case, right? That's what I told myself, but nothing in life prepared me for the bedlam I'm about to face. Despite the craziness, the chases and the unexpected fighting, I need to solve

this thing to justify my employment.
Unfortunately, I have no idea what I am doing, I'm still working my
notice period in the police, and I have a date tonight.

I'll find the ghost, be sure of it, but why, oh why, did I invite sassy BFF
Patience Woods to help out.

Get ready for snark-fuelled fun as Amanda Harper goes ghostbusting!

More Books by Steve Higgs

Blue Moon Investigations

Paranormal Nonsense

The Phantom of Barker Mill

Amanda Harper Paranormal Detective

The Klowns of Kent

Dead Pirates of Cawsand

In the Doodoo With Voodoo

The Witches of East Malling

Crop Circles, Cows and Crazy Aliens

Whispers in the Rigging

Bloodlust Blonde – a short story

Paws of the Yeti

Under a Blue Moon – A Paranormal Detective Origin Story

Night Work

Lord Hale's Monster

The Herne Bay Howlers

Undead Incorporated

The Ghoul of Christmas Past

Patricia Fisher Cruise Mysteries

The Missing Sapphire of Zangrabar

The Kidnapped Bride

The Director's Cut

The Couple in Cabin 2124

Doctor Death

Murder on the Dancefloor

Mission for the Maharaja

A Sleuth and her Dachshund in Athens

The Maltese Parrot

No Place Like Home

Patricia Fisher Mystery Adventures

What Sam Knew

Solstice Goat

Recipe for Murder

A Banshee and a Bookshop

Diamonds, Dinner Jackets, and Death

Frozen Vengeance

Mug Shot

The Godmother

Murder is an Artform

Wonderful Weddings and Deadly Divorces

Albert Smith Culinary Capers

Pork Pie Pandemonium

Bakewell Tart Bludgeoning

Stilton Slaughter

Bedfordshire Clanger Calamity

Death of a Yorkshire Pudding

Cumberland Sausage Shocker

Arbroath Smokie Slaying

Free Books and More

Get sneak peaks, exclusive giveaways, behind the scenes content, and more. Plus, you'll be notified of Fan Pricing events when they occur and get exclusive offers from other authors because all UF writers are automatically friends.

Not only that, but you'll receive an exclusive FREE story staring Otto and Zachary and two free stories from the author's Blue Moon Investigations series.

Yes, please! Sign me up for lots of FREE stuff and bargains!

Want to follow me and keep up with what I am doing?

Facebook

Printed in Great Britain
by Amazon

55188885R00140